# SCAPEGOATS & CROWBARS

*A collection of short stories*

ELIAS PELL

Scapegoats & Crowbars
Elias Pell

Cover Design by: Unfamiliar Spirits

First Edition 2020

ISBN-10: 1-91634-460-0

ISBN-13: 978-1-91634-460-0

**Alliance,** n. In international politics, the union of two thieves who have their hands so deeply inserted in each other's pockets that they cannot separately plunder a third.

*Ambrose Bierce - The Devil's Dictionary.*

**Neighbor,** n. One whom we are commanded to love as ourselves, and does all he knows how to make us disobedient.

*Ambrose Bierce - The Devil's Dictionary.*

# CONTENTS


Introduction *by Elias Pell* xi

The Nostalgic Landlord 1

A Light at the Middle of the Tunnel 3

The Chimera of Migration *(plus Author's Notes)* 7

Out of Touch 13

The Line Between Conrad and Goebbels 15

Wide-eyed Scrying 24

An Apple Falling 26

Bodie, the Bucket List & the Body Snatchers 30

Organic Defences 48

World of Shadows 52

The Cruelest Cohabitation 61

Bound by the Greater Good 63

Two Wrongs Just Might...? 67

The Questionable Corpse 75

Served Cold 78

Needle in a Haystack 80

A Shot in the Dark 89

The Subliminal Compass 91

DNR, SOS 101

Confessions of a Serial Killer 104

Of a Feather 108

To Infinity and Beyond 125

Special thanks to my first readers: Beata, Michael, Lucia, Daniel, Anne and Alistair. Without their incredible patience, feedback and encouragement this collection might never have come about.

Last, and certainly not least, a massive thank you to my current Patrons, whose generosity and faith in my work keeps me pushing forward through setbacks and moments of self-doubt:

Alan Lee
Ozan Fahri
Anne Matthews
Lucia Nieto

# INTRODUCTION

*BY ELIAS PELL*

The stories contained in this collection were written in 2018. Having just finished my first YA novel, *Steggie Belle & the Dream Warriors*, and having been lucky enough to sign a contract with a publisher straight away, I thought I would take a few months and try my hand at short stories. Things somewhat ballooned from there. After unexpectedly winning an international competition, and having two stories published, on the encouragement of several readers, I decided to release *Scapegoats & Crowbars* to a—hopefully—wider audience.

Perhaps here, it would be a good idea for me to give a little explanation of my thoughts behind the title. The original working title *"The Crookedness of Scapegoats & The Curvature of Crowbars"* was, I have been repeatedly told, even more obscure. Animals are incorporated in many of my stories, including my two previously published ones: in *Timeo Danaos*, a new species of jellyfish mysteriously washes up dead with the tide, and humanity is not prepared for the consequences that follow. And in *White Elephants Remain*, the story follows a homeless man and his dog as they cling to one another in the final, bizarre hours leading up to the end of the world. Both of these stories were meant to be included within *Scapegoats & Crowbars* but sadly, due to contractual reasons, cannot be at the present time.

So, why the goat and the crow? Well, simply put, both of these animals have long been associated with evil: goats, with sin and Satan himself; crows, commonly stereotyped as villains and the foretellers of death.

The two title words' compounds: 'scape' (an archaic verb meaning "escape") and 'bars', conjure images of flight and freedom, of confinement and imprisonment. Taken in their complete form, both words appeared to me to resonate with a deep social relevance within our current times.

Throughout history, it seems that human beings have had a tendency of looking for scapegoats: someone to blame when faced with hard times, irrespective of that person's or group's innocence or guilt. The word's origin, from Leviticus, tells the story of a goat being selected and cast out into the desert, to carry away people's sins and thus cleanse the community.

In this modern, technological age of instant communication, combined with the deliberate, powerful spread of misinformation and the threat of economic and climatic disasters looming, I worry that there may never have been as dangerous a time for the viral selection of future scapegoats.

Along such topical lines, in *The Chimera of Migration*, the subjects of instinctive racial profiling and the power of paranoia are examined, when an airline stewardess faces an impossible dilemma under extreme pressure. *Organic Defences* attempts, through the use of abstract allegories, to raise questions about the problems of alterity ("otherness") in a closed society and the building of impenetrable walls. While in *Confessions of a Serial Killer*, on an environmental note, plastic itself is given a chance to defend its 'bad name'.

Which brings us to crowbars: a simple, useful tool used to pry things open by force. The question is how such an instrument will be used, and for what intent? Will it be used to break down divisive barriers—both psychological and physical—and unite people in acceptance of the differences we share? Or will it be used to rip and tear apart the fragile bonds which link humanity together? As a tool of liberation, or as a blunt, lethal weapon causing more destruction and suffering?

Growing up, I always favoured the underdog: I remember watching, waiting patiently until a player would concede at chess, before approaching the table and asking if I could continue in their place. Sadly, my level of chess is amateur at best, so most often the result remained unchanged: defeat is sometimes inevitable, but hope—even against the odds—is something I struggle to simply abandon. Life, however, with its colourful yet indifferent way of dealing out experiences, has succeeded—I must admit—in sullying my youthful optimism to some degree.

But, as a wise man once told me, "It is not what happens to a person, but rather how they react, that makes them the way they are." Although this, in my opinion, is one of the factors that make our species not the highest and most evolved animal on Earth, but by far the most dangerous.

This idea of personal transformation is recurrent throughout the collection. In *The Line Between Conrad & Goebbels*, the story follows a young boy playing make-believe. It suggests that these subtle psychological changes might occur quite unseen, drastically altering even a very young individual's potential path. It examines age-old questions of Nature vs Nurture, the corruptive influence of power, and whether or not we are actually in complete control of our decisions: the life balance between Good and Evil; becoming men or monsters. *An Apple Falling* witnesses one man's internal struggle against the temptation of descending into the nightmarish footsteps of his past. While, in *The Questionable Corpse*, a young woman is forced to confront her 'true self', and see through her own mental delusions, when an unexpected event causes her past, present and future to collide.

Perhaps, in this collection of stories, my general cynicism might appear overpowering at times, bordering even on pessimism. However, somewhere below the surface, I believe the dwindling embers of romanticism and hope are still burning.

Lastly, I would like to thank you, the reader, sincerely and welcome you as a friend to my imagination. I am deeply indebted to you for your support and hope that someday, in some way our paths might cross so I can return the favour. All proceeds from this collection of short stories will be reinvested into future writing projects: the first being the publication of my debut novel, *Steggie Belle & the Dream Warriors.* Please, do check my website for updates, and to find out more:

www.eliaspell.com

More than anything, it is my humble hope that you will enjoy these stories of mine and find something worthwhile within these pages.

# THE NOSTALGIC LANDLORD

He enjoyed these quiet moments, the tranquil in-betweens after the dust had settled: time to speculate, to reflect.

The cleaning crews would arrive soon, to wipe away all trace of what had gone before, priming the place into yet another blank canvas. There was very little for him to do, no need to place an advert, with the current climate it was a property owner's paradise: the void would quickly be filled.

The last tenants had been a rarity indeed, quite unlike any he had dealt with previously. He had long regarded himself as a benevolent proprietor, easy-going and open-minded, but they had pushed his patience to new extremes.

He had certainly underestimated how many of them were intending to move in. He had learnt his lesson, making a mental note to enquire next time or stipulate reasonable limits somewhere within the contract.

They had been strangely gregarious: simultaneously needy and dismissive. Had bred like rabbits, and yet somehow never really seemed to get along. Always new faces appearing under that same one roof.

Nevertheless, he had liked the former tenants, although he

often suspected the feeling was not mutual. Yes, they had been noisy, unruly and gluttonous to the core, but boy could they cook!

Natural creativity had caused them to be obsessed with making incessant alterations, but—he supposed in retrospect—that had been part and parcel of their charm. A genuine desire and desperation to improve their surroundings and, in so doing, perhaps themselves. So many sentimental trinkets to which they had seemed so devoted, and yet they had left them all behind. Maybe they would return, at some later date, for all those belongings, though he remained doubtful of that.

Considering—in the grand scheme of things—how short their stay had been, they had left an impressive mess in their wake. Definitely forfeiting their deposit. Besides, having departed so suddenly, in their haste they had forgotten to even leave a forwarding address.

The cockroach wondered to himself who the next tenants would be, scuttling unassumingly through the endless rubble and ash.

# A LIGHT AT THE MIDDLE OF THE TUNNEL

First impressions had been promising. Dark tunnel. Distant light. The feeling of floating weightlessly towards it. Being sucked into one of the tunnel wall fixtures had come as a surprise. It hadn't taken long to deduce the locale, only minutes before the first rumbling train thundered through.

Instinctively he knew his body was gone, how else could he be stuck inside a light bulb? Some misrepresented Heaven? Or feebly imagined Hell? Unsure, he waited—like a tourist in some unfathomably foreign land—for answers. They never came.

As far as potential afterlives go, it wasn't so bad. He was impressed by the sheer recyclable frugality of it all. It took some getting used to, of course. The lack of any certitude he found most infuriating but then, having lived as an atheist, he couldn't really complain. The biggest hurdle was boredom: how best to occupy a disembodied mind.

The sole distraction were those passing trains. He found that he possessed a new talent. Here, time was flexible, with practice and focus he could slow down those shuttling carriages to a snail's pace, viewing the passengers within frame by frame.

Doing so, he discovered these were not the Underground tunnels of London, but Rome. Another mystery: since his living body had never been there. His only connection to the city was that Mary had often begged that they should go; a romantic getaway, anniversary visit, or better yet a much needed fresh start.

Being the filament within some Roman light bulb had distressed him a great deal at first. Perhaps it was the guilty feeling of abandonment, having left Mary all alone. Another failing on his part. He had never meant to hurt her, or cause her pain; had just wanted the best for her, even if she seldom understood his possessive methods of expression. He thought of her often. How, when his terminal prognosis was made, she had wept. How Mary had promised—despite all his protestations—that she would never love again. He hadn't pushed the matter: but now with ample time and absolute honesty, he realised he had been delighted, overjoyed at her eternal pledge. His life had not been meaningless, his fragile ego relieved that truly he had been her world. In a London tunnel, there would have been at least a chance that her path might cross his prison cell. He had imagined the scene often: of her grief-stricken and in mourning, then maybe a faint and fleeting smile across her face, at the remembrance of a time they had shared.

Such longshot probabilities equal loneliness. Yet, 'When in Rome...' as the old saying goes. He had, therefore, decided even without the hope of seeing Mary, to take an active interest in his surroundings. Every train was delicately spiced and laden with stories: every carriage a melting pot of emotions and jaundiced dreams. He became a voyeur. Coveting their little daily dramas, their exquisite lives rolling repetitively by.

There was only one other distraction down in that dark tunnel. The far rarer and unpredictable appearance of some maintenance man: forever whistling the same lifeless tune. Most often simply checking the tracks, but on one occasion, swapping out a 'dead' bulb. Seeing that got him thinking seriously.

He learnt the real power of faith. After all, with too much time and solitude, general reasoning can often lead to unambiguous convictions. He did the maths. Logic confirmed that this stasis could not be a permanent arrangement. The tunnel had to be some sort of staging area, a waiting room for some inevitable transition—perhaps better known by the living as Limbo or Purgatory. Surely, he surmised, his next life was destined to begin in Italy. He liked that idea: practised to perfection the phrase 'Ciao bella!' from inside of his cocoon.

Time ticked with the rhythmic passing of trains. Then, quite unexpectedly, one day, it happened. At first he convinced himself it wasn't her, couldn't possibly be. Mary looked so different. Over their last ten years together, he had not allowed her, nor had she ever once dared to step outside in anything but long sleeves, sunglasses and scarf. All covered up, no matter what the weather. Heavy makeup hiding the consequences of her terrible 'clumsiness', her freshly bruised flesh a testament to the fact that she never listened to him, and would never learn.

Now, seeing her in a vest top and summer skirt, he barely recognised her. He couldn't remember her skin ever looking so healthy. She was smiling too—no—beaming in fact, her cheeks all rosy and flushed. Then he saw she was not alone. The equally cheerful man she was standing next to was raising his arm, in a slow-motion and terrible arc. Was he about to strike her, or to wrap it protectively around her shoulder? Mary did not flinch at all—yet another inconsistency from the woman he had known. Then they were gone. The next carriages no longer offered any interest or amusement for him. He could feel his temper rising, that fusion of fear and anger flowing.

Creating an unstable current and causing an emotional lapse of self-control.

Filaments really are such fragile things.

Soon afterwards, still wavering between denial and disbelief, there came the sound of that distant whistling.

As the workman drew near, he noticed one light bulb flickering erratically. He waited for a while in the hope it was just some temporary malfunction, then altered his direction and approached the faulty bulb. The tunnel was deathly silent. As he unscrewed it, he could not hear the frantic screaming from within.

Now, inside that bulb, only darkness. An eternity for a trapped soul to do battle with itself. Tormented by the enigma: what was the worst it could have been?

# THE CHIMERA OF MIGRATION

"Don't you dare! If you give up, we're all going to die!"

Sadly it was a redundant demand since the co-pilot was also dead. The stewardess shook him one last time for good measure, before claustrophobia set in. The world was shrinking, the cockpit small.

He had tried to gurgle something while convulsing and turning blue: 'Poisoned' or 'Poisonous' perhaps, but she couldn't be sure. Had thrust a ripped scrap of paper to her, in that final death spasm. The beginning of a word, four letters scrawled before the jagged tear:

'Terr—'.

Mentally she paced, in reality, she simply trembled. Those two qualified and capable dead men sitting rigid, with their glassy-eyed stares, fixed on that predictable horizon. Surrounded by a staggering number of dials, buttons and switches. Too many choices to be left to unacquainted chance. Nervously she checked the instruments.

Altitude: terrifyingly high.

Speed: incomprehensibly fast.

Fuel: guaranteed finitude.

Those she recognised, most of the others remained a mystery.

Autopilot: engaged.

Good, she thought. Much better that something else was temporarily in control, albeit an artificial responsibility. She glanced out the window, then instantly regretted doing so.

Visibility: abysmal. Hurtling through the endless cloud cover at 505 mph, and flying blind into the night.

Behind her came a muffled knocking from the aircraft cabin.

"Don't think about it," she told herself. Too late; her mind now becoming distracted by the thoughts and faces of the other crew and the hundred-plus passengers onboard. "Oh, God, the children."

"Make it sound minor, break it to them gently, in manageable, bite-sized pieces," she reassured herself, before pressing the intercom.

The conversation was clipped, more an interrogation from her colleague on the other side. A series of vague white-lies spiralling their slippery descent toward the inevitable truth.

'Taken ill' had sounded good. 'Incapacitated' had not gone down so well. 'Both deceased' even worse. Thick insulation thankfully dampened the panic that followed on the other side of the door.

"The radio!" she gasped, prying the headset off the nearest corpse. The tuned frequency was worrying.

Thousands of voices, with their brief messages shooting over one another. Contradictory opinions, all claiming to hold the truth. A shrill cacophony of confusion, an infinite brood collectively warbling for attention. No trustworthy answers were to be found within that raging sea of anonymity.

More urgent rapping upon the cockpit door.

"We've found a passenger who has experience with aircraft, says he can fly the plane."

The stewardess peered closer at the grainy little screen.

Almost hidden behind the pale and anxious cabin crew, the other man. A snapshot image, just a dozen pixels to cast judgement. She squinted hard. His skin looked darker, his eyes foreign.

A crossword lover she was not, but her mind automatically filled in the blanks. Two words flashed red, like the Fasten Seatbelt sign: 'Terrorism' and 'Terrorist'. All other possibilities evaporated.

A crossroads now: direct communication versus abstract reasoning. The stewardess backed away from the intercom, returning to the radio. Out of the chaotic static, one crisp, cold voice patching through.

"Don't let them in!"

Was that Air Traffic Control? Some airline official? Should she trust the unknown speaker? Obey his command?

"Identify yourself," she pleaded. The same heartless order rebounded back.

More noises from outside now. Frantic cries quickly rising, and a heavy, dull, metallic pounding.

"Open the bloody door!" she recognised that voice.

The screen showed a crowd had now amassed out there: writhing like sardines, piled within a cramped tin can. A tide of desperate bodies washing up, slamming against the reinforced door.

She was crying now.

Somewhere an alarm was sounding. Her moral compass spinning; magnetic north was gone. Caught between two opposing mantras booming, resounding, chiming like cathedral bells.

"Don't let them in!" echoing out of the dangling headset, in an authoritative and indifferent tone.

"Let us in!" the chorus of despair from beyond the barrier.

The stewardess never thought to reach over and check the

co-pilot's clenched fist. Never found the second part to his word of warning: '—itorialism'. Would it have mattered, or made any difference? Was it just a twisted metaphor conjured by her subconscious mind, clawing for the surface?

At what point do logic and objectivity part ways when confronted with the shine of a guillotine's blade? How to balance thoughts of victims, children and future generations, against the weight of present suffering?

Survival, perhaps the most powerful and basic instinct: to protect one's place amongst the living. Staring down the barrel of a gun, aren't we all refugees of one kind or another? Transitory migrants holding onto some threadbare hope, rattling against whatever border fences we find, begging for mercy. To be tamed or made—checked or mated.

The stewardess exhaled slowly and said a prayer. Her fingers hesitating over the lock.

# AUTHOR'S NOTES FOR THE CHIMERA OF MIGRATION

In this story, I wanted to create an impossible dilemma under immense pressure: one with imminent danger and without room to breathe. The locked cockpit of a commercial aircraft seemed perfectly claustrophobic. The mystery of the two dead pilots and the clues they left behind are quickly eclipsed by the fact that nobody with knowledge is flying the plane.

The "instruments", the situation, all a metaphor for humanity's current global predicament: soaring up and out into the great unknown at a truly terrifying speed, with limited resources, and nobody in control. The "five-hundred and five miles per hour" reading (S.O.S), as the aircraft continues ahead on auto-pilot: a subtle cry for help.

The door to the cockpit becomes the final safety barrier, the last wall of separation. The stewardess's only hope for reasoned advice is from the radio: the "shrill cacophony" "warbling for attention," referring to the anonymity of Social Media and Twitter; the inescapable confusion, amid the escalating spread of misinformation, as to who or what we should believe.

Her judgement—based on limited physical appearances and stereotyping—is inevitably flawed.

The possible saviour, on the other side, who might be able to land the plane, could very well be linked to the Terr-orist who has Poisoned the two pilots.

The actual message—that it was in fact "Poisonous Territorialism"—is forever lost in that moment. The question of what it really means to be a migrant is raised with hope.

It is one which begs objectivity: that perhaps it is a quality within our very nature—being the transient owners of these bodies of ours, always looking to improve our own situation while moving around this planet we like to call "our home." *The Chimera of Migration*, in the end, boils down to her final, desperate decision: whether or not to unlock and open the cockpit door?

# OUT OF TOUCH

"I blame those artists!" the grandmother concluded.

"He's a good boy, dear, never abuses the privileges of his generation," the grandfather replied soothingly, settling back into the armchair and most likely—she suspected—switching off his hearing aid.

"Well, you shouldn't encourage him anyway," she continued undeterred, "always asking him for details about those music parties."

"Raves," her husband corrected, his eyes now closed.

There came the sound of a key scratching around in the front door lock.

"He's here, thank God. Arrested; really, at his age!"

She shuffled out into the hallway. The grandfather re-opened one eye cautiously.

"You must be starving, I'll fetch some biscuits. Digestives, not those 'star cakes' mind!"

"Space Cakes, grandma." the young man laughed, entering the sitting room.

The elderly man listened intently as his grandson explained all that had happened: 'Picked up for questioning. Person of interest. Circumstantial evidence.'

"This 'Hippie Strangler' struck after all the last events I went to, appears to select and stalk his victims from there. Except; you remember the one that I told you about last Saturday, well I… ended up making other plans.

"That lucky coincidence became my alibi; otherwise, they'd probably still be interrogating me down at the station, taking blood, DNA and all sorts."

The grandfather nodded meditatively, hiding his concern.

"Why would somebody do this grandpa? He's murdered seven randoms already."

"Maybe jealousy?" the grandfather hypothesised, interlocking his fingers. "You see, growing up in my day we didn't have all these distractions: luxuries of drugs; liberation of sex. Our existence was more straightforward and limited. Perhaps the killer's envious? Believes they're misusing those privileges, self-indulgently taking them for granted?"

"Bitterness is hardly a motive, grandpa…" he chose his next words carefully, avoiding terms like 'depraved' and 'perverted', or other graphic modernisms that might unsettle the old man.

"The police think it's some sort of fetish," he paused again, sympathetic towards his grandfather's clueless expression. "Besides, I didn't really fit their profile."

"Profile?"

"Yes, grandpa. It's what they do nowadays: white male, twenty-five to forty, thorough knowledge of chemical sedatives."

The grandfather raised an inquisitive eyebrow.

"Wouldn't that make me a 'person of interest' then?"

"Perhaps forty years ago, grandpa!" he scoffed, laughing fondly at the harmless, long-retired chemist who was drifting off to sleep across from him.

The grandfather had closed his eyes again, smiling peacefully. Content that he was still in the clear.

# THE LINE BETWEEN CONRAD AND GOEBBELS

It was that magical hour before suppertime when parents are kept busy and have a habit of turning their backs. He crept silent and unseen along the garden path, past the graveyard vegetable patch, towards the edge of civilisation where the wildlands began. Crouching low at the edge of the clearing, he examined the telltale soil for tracks. His crooked wooden rifle at the ready, and white-knuckled index finger curled around that invisible trigger. Gripped by that giddying, instinctive sensation that he was not alone.

Up ahead to his left stood that lonely pagan shrine. Its ancient frame entwined in serpentine coils of ivy, a stranglehold that would one day drag the entire structure beneath the ground, and back to hell. By day it masqueraded as a simple woodshed, yet only he was privy to its terrible past. Centuries of ceremonies, blood sacrifices and devilry had conjured something truly diabolical: a beast with an insatiable taste for the living that skulked and roamed the great beyond.

The young boy made a sudden break for cover, reaching the outbuilding quickly and slamming one shoulder up against the spongy, mould covered timber corner-post. There he hesitated, heart pounding as he squinted down that slightly twisted barrel, casting furtive glances in all directions. At length, emboldened by the fact that he had not been followed, the boy retreated tentatively towards the shadows behind the woodshed.

It was a secret place into which he crawled, a narrow alley running between the back of that ramshackle building and the tall wooden fence. Damp and difficult was the path, despite his slim physique, that led to the lookout point. The kind of claustrophobic place that adults deem unworthy and only children see real value. It was a test of will to run that gauntlet, pushing through the ashes and bones of those brave adventurers who had gone before. Clambering over curious piles of long discarded relics, and under silken tripwires spun back and forth at cruel and devious angles. Through curtains of overhanging creepers with their razorblade tendrils reaching down, feigning dormancy and most probably poisonous.

As he pulled and shimmied his way along, he pondered the future. Whether someday, perhaps by the unimaginably distant milestone of his tenth birthday, his body might actually grow to betray him and forbid him access to that favourite hiding place. "Impossible," he whispered defiantly to his brain, having successfully managed to reach the spot.

He checked that everything was exactly as he had left it, before taking his seat on an upturned wooden crate. That cramped passage ended quite abruptly at the farthest corner of the woodshed, where a waist-high crumbling stone wall rose up to block the exit. A semi-circular barrier between the perimeter fence and side of the building which created a small enclosure, protected from all outside threats. The boy hastily prepared himself, laying the rifle carefully atop of that low rampart and rooting through his modestly furnished fort. He propped the curved sabre within arm's reach up against the shed, and placed his trusted duelling pistol across his lap, before nestling the rifle-butt back into his shoulder.

With winter coming, his view through the lifeless, leafless undergrowth was mostly unobstructed, and he waited with the patience of a seasoned hunter, his senses finely tuned to the unpredictable world around him. He steadied his breathing, until only the faintest frozen plume escaped his lips, evanescing like a silent prayer.

He knew, despite sworn assurances to the contrary, that monsters did exist. They were everywhere and nowhere, and seldom to be caught out in the open. Not the mythological sort, which grown-up rationality could so easily dismiss, but a far more subtle and sinister kind. Though the boy was only eight years old, he had already witnessed plenty. Instances of possession and that sudden flash within familiar eyes, momentary contortions of the face as the monster took ahold of the host. Rarely did they remain long inside one individual; only enough time to spark havoc, before shifting unnoticed into the next victim. Like evil puppet masters pulling strings, leaving pain and devastation in their wake: the modern world their canvas; mankind their brush; creating grim strokes and woeful patterns within the chaos.

That evening he was hunting their leader. The monster who had recently left a strange footprint upon the garden path. When the boy first found it, he knew it was a warning that the household had been marked. It would soon be coming for his parents, for them all. Which had led him there, aiming his rifle with the one unquestionably flawless and virtuous intention: to protect his family.

To confirm his theory of the existence of an unseen world, the boy picked up a large flat stone and turned it over in his hand. He watched the orgy of insects scuttling and slithering in all directions, panicked by the sudden disturbance. Nodding with satisfaction, he laid that weighty marquee—their city roof—carefully back down, turning his attention once more to the rifle sights.

Shivering in the advancing twilight, he noticed that small crystals of frost had begun to form on the rough fabric of his overcoat, glittering like rhinestone sequins. From somewhere nearby came the distinctive smell of damp leaves smouldering from a garden heap. The heady scent of Autumn's ruin, but there was an underlying sweetness within such death and decay.

Suddenly the sound of footsteps, faint at first, but drawing near. Terrified, the boy tightened his grip in expectation, not moving a muscle, even when the giant figure came into view. It was his father, marching with recognisable haste and frustration he knew only too well. A matter of adult importance was clearly on his mind, as he paced about outside the woodshed, inhaling bitterly upon his cigarette, and exhaling in exasperation.

Automatically the boy swung the barrel around and steadied his aim. He squeezed the trigger twice in quick succession: one shot to the heart, one to the head. His father neither flinched nor fell. Then the most extraordinary thing happened. That hulk of a man—seemingly unaware of the assassination attempt—suddenly broke down and cried. For a moment, the boy looked down in awe at his weapon. Irredeemable guilt flooded his brain from that first act of patricide, but those feelings soon transformed. Surprise and disbelief solidifying into an unforgiving rage. 'Hypocrite!' was the scream on the very tip of his tongue. The boy's eyes narrowed, and his lip began to tremble.

The family dog appeared from nowhere and sidled up beside his master. With a look of concern and a pitying whine, the devoted animal rubbed up against the father's leg: a rudimentary attempt to comfort. The father stared down at the dog, and it was then the boy saw it. The man's eyes changed, corrupted in an instant as the monster took hold. A sharp kick sent the dog tumbling, retreating back towards the house with a yelp and his tail between his legs.

The boy retook aim.

Before he could fire, his target tossed the cigarette away and stormed inside the shed, noisily gathering up a bucket full of firewood. Only once his father had disappeared back up the garden path, did the boy's hands start to shake uncontrollably, caught in the whirlpool vertigo of an adrenaline rush. Through the tears, he told himself it was only the cold. Distraction was necessary to avoid that bare-faced lie, so he focused on a spiderweb delicately stretched out between branches on the other side of the wall. Its creator was silhouetted at the orb web's epicentre, positioned like some stately lord at the head of the banquet table, waiting for his next meal to arrive.

The boy considered an arachnid's existence. Whether that strategic predatory lifestyle was in fact so very different from his species' own? He had heard somewhere that they were cannibals, but then again he had just hunted down and mentally murdered his own father. Patient and calculating, they would spin their webs, without the need for conscience or mercy towards their prey. Some were poisonous, though if he were to believe his mother, the same was true of men. The more he thought about it, the more similarities and comparisons he was able to find. From the potential to create such mesmerising and beautiful designs, to a kindred capacity to terrify and cause alarm. He recalled some vague memory of grown-ups passionately discussing politicians and their never-ending webs of lies. This reasoning all led him to a crux: was that correlation of temperament something for a child to aspire to? Even he could foresee that in this world not everybody could be the spider. Some people would have to be the fly.

Daylight was fading fast, and the boy shuddered at the thought of those molten dark shadows melding into one another, creeping out of every corner and flooding the whole house. It would be a long and perilous journey to the safety of his bed. Reciting prayers beneath the covers, warding off the night until sleep would carry him away. In his dreams, he was protected and able to soar high above the limitations of this world. Time and again, he experienced moments of clarity within those dreams, guided by voices who insisted he was special. Who assured him that his life held great purpose; that his words would one day command both influence and power. Promises of some splendid destiny. He found, upon waking that his heart was both elated and daunted by such possibilities.

He remembered once confiding those innermost secrets to his mother. Though it was her reaction which had been entirely unexpected, rooting itself so deeply in his memory. She had listened intently as he spoke, before turning away, he assumed to consider the meaning of those dreams of his. When she looked back, however, he noticed the tears in her eyes. It was empathy that had made his own eyes follow suit, and she had held him close for what seemed an eternity. Was it some maternal wisdom that caused her to cry? Perhaps a dreadful fear that the modern world was too harsh and cruel, or he too sensitive, too much of a dreamer to survive it? Or could it have been the fear that he may have been right? Whatever her reason, she never said a word.

The silent embrace was only broken by his father entering the room. No questions had been asked, but one angry lesson had been swiftly beaten into him right then and there. Every strike of his father's hand dealt with disdain. "Boys don't cry!"

He had stayed silent, bitten his lip and made no excuses. He saw himself drowning then within the incoherent swells of love and hate. Somewhere between his heart and mind, at that moment, a wall was being raised, a shell slowly thickening into granite.

Yet now, behind that woodshed, he had just witnessed a chink in his father's armour, the weakness of hypocrisy. He could feel raw anger stirring inside of him, and raised his eyes up towards the ever-darkening sky, hoping it would pass.

Directly over his head, dangling like the sword of Damocles, hung an empty cocoon swaying weightlessly on the breeze. He raised himself to examine it more closely. It was nothing but a fragile husk, whose freshly winged former tenant had long since burst free and taken to the sky. The boy glanced back and forth between the spider and the cocoon and wondered whether Fate could have been so cruel. It made him think of the scab upon his knee, still sore from a fall he had taken two days before. He wondered if it all could be connected. Whether life could simply be a continuous and painful learning curve? A necessary tearing and repetitive shedding of skin, from which a unique and solitary adult would emerge? The greatest mystery, a gamble played by every man and woman, waiting to see what scars would eventually form. An isolated world of Calibans crouching fearfully in their caves; hiding from the inevitability of progress and change. Avoiding the tempestuous desires of both the men and monsters that awaited them, should they ever find the courage to step outside?

In the distance, the local church bells chimed out their hollow forebodings to both the living and the dead. The boy turned the pistol over in his lap, assessing the odds and the feasibility of somehow stopping time. If there could be a way of staying there forever and never going back.

Another frightful sound rang out across the encroaching night. A demented mating call whose rasping and desperate cry perfectly resembled a young woman being strangled.

Out of that momentary paralytic terror, the boy's eyes then fell upon a long column of ants, navigating an epic trail along the top of that stone wall. Their movement was sluggish yet regimented, battling the cold for supplies one final time before hibernation. The boy edged closer, working his way along that uniformed and marching army with growing curiosity. There was a rotting piece of bark blocking their path, immovable as some colossal mountain range. He sensed their quandary as they reached it, and marvelled at their predictable nature, striking the same route around the obstacle to the exact point upon the other side, before continuing on their way.

He was struck suddenly by the godlike power at his fingertips. How, with one simple movement, he could clear their path and alter their destiny. He imagined they would tell stories for aeons to come about the hero who had moved a mountain just for them. The boy placed the pistol down, determined to become their saviour, and reached forward with one giant hand. At the last second, he paused, hesitating on the very verge of greatness. Some subconscious thought steered his hand away, drew it back to the ground in a dizzying arc of spontaneity. His fingers returned from those shadowed depths firmly grasping that flat, cold stone.

The underside was still swarming with all manner of insects, and as he raised it high above that wall, he felt the pulsation of a very different kind of power. He was all that stood between two worlds colliding and being crushed beyond repair. The scales seemed unbalanced: brutality more enchanting than aspiring towards some higher moral code. In that soul defining moment, not a single monster in the world dared even draw breath. His eyes had changed. The scab was peeling away.

A familiar sound caught his attention, as he wavered on the edge of that abyss. The back door opening and his mother's voice calling out to him.

"Joseph! Supper's ready."

Straining under the intensity of that pressure, the boy released the stone. Racing away with the crooked rifle in his hands, he ran for his life all the way along that winding garden path. Retreating from his heart. Retreating from the darkness.

# WIDE-EYED SCRYING

## *IN THE SPIRIT OF COMMUNICATION*

Deep breath. This won't be like last time. Still, he should have made more effort to learn the language. Nothing but a blind orgy of useless words canoodling ineffectively around his head. The cringe-worthy memory returns:

*The hospital. His girlfriend being wheeled off to the anaesthetist. Her mother's worry was only broken by anger, at seeing her husband already dozing. Of him being stuck there in the middle. Wishing he could trade places and be on that gurney. It's raining heavily outside. An ominous roll of thunder as he sees her mother pull that other-worldly object from her bag. Her laying it ritualistically between them. Her concentration assures him that it's going to be a long two hours. He closes his eyes, doesn't want to see her hands moving mystically over the device—its reflective surface with its bewitching blue glow. Then he hears that voice: dreadfully cold and inhumanly disjointed, communicating from that other realm. His turn now—he knows it. The inescapable silence awaiting his reply.*

Deep breath. This time it'll be different. He's in control. Besides, they've bonded since then. Reassured, he pulls out his own more modern and superior device. His girlfriend is not there: that's the reason for this, after all. Her parents eye him suspiciously, perhaps fearful of the message they will receive?

Surely they knew this day would come? His turn now, to start this ritual of theirs.

Deep breath. Looking down with arms outstretched, his fingers begin to move. He types with care and precision on the smartphone. Double-checks that autocorrect has not betrayed him. His index finger lingers over that fateful symbol. The one next to it resembles a blackened, pestilence-ridden head of corn, or worse still, a decapitated man. Google Translate promises that it's just a microphone. He presses the sound button instead: no going back now. That same lifeless yet foreign voice is conjured instantly. Then silence. His mind fixates upon the absurd. He wonders whether asking for a daughter's hand in marriage sounds even stranger in Swahili? Time to test that and change the language setting later.

Her father looks stunned. Her mother reaches hastily for the device. Starts typing her response with great enthusiasm it seems. Although—he notices—she's not smiling. Her eyes filled with a passion that looks a little more like anger.

Oh, God. Deep breath.

# AN APPLE FALLING

He should never have gone. He knew that now.

The dead tend to hold a monopoly on legacies, often rewriting history.

"A good man—your father," the Executor commented. Michael refused to cry, dug his fingernails into his palms until they bled.

"Misunderstood by many, I fear," he continued while scanning the Will.

Michael nodded uncomfortably.

It was a simple process: with Michael the only related beneficiary; and the rest of the estate left to a children's charity.

"Such a fondness for those poor, unfortunate little ones," the Executor concluded, pushing the carved wooden box across the desk. Michael nodded again, his eyes transfixed upon that item bequeathed.

Peculiar to be left an antique locked box without a key.

When probed as to what it might contain, Michael lied.

"Only my father's photographs and sentimental keepsakes."

The Executor eyed him dubiously, suspecting priceless heirlooms probably lay inside. The man had no idea…

Once the papers were signed, Michael headed for the nearest pub where, within a secluded corner, he nursed his pint meditatively for hours. There, as suppressed memories resurfaced, he wept quietly.

His father repetitively pounding special lessons into him from a young age. Squeezing his shoulder affectionately afterwards. Leaning over from behind to whisper his favourite motto in Michael's ear: "Carpe Diem!" before releasing him outside to play. His mother's final words before she abandoned them, begging him to be strong, to believe in himself.

His fingers trailed absent-mindedly over the contours of the old box. He wanted so badly to believe. Convinced himself at that point to try one last time, to risk vulnerability in order to rejoin the light-heartedness of the human race. With a little liquid courage and 'Carpe Diem' on his lips—conquering his chronic shyness—he approached a pretty girl at the bar. Smooth-talking failed him spectacularly. Mortified, he retreated to his corner, bitterly humiliated as the girl and her friends laughed. A cruel weapon, the world's laughter: poisonous and seeping through his skin. He desired invisibility or oblivion, would have flipped a coin for it and taken either outcome graciously.

His clammy hand withdrew a length of leather cord from beneath his shirt. For too many years it had been hanging like a noose around his neck. Tied to its end, terribly cold to the touch: the key.

Another flashback memory: creeping through the house before dawn on his sixteenth birthday. The dilemma of whether to steal the box itself, finally settling more perniciously for the key. He had left his home running and never looked back, reassuring himself that his little sister would be fine: father never cared much for her anyhow.

Nothing seemed real anymore. Michael's entire being felt

fractured. His individuality a vase, cracking into a thousand pieces. Extreme fragility, threatening to shatter completely at even the slightest touch.

A surge of hopeless isolation swept over him. With his sense of social affinity diminishing and feeling ostracised by sobriety, he studied that sea of smiling faces. Those inebriated, merry loons leering out from under fake candlelight.

A violent gale rattled the windowpane, needle-like rain lashing as lightning ripped the blackened sky. It was a night where surely—in some gothic loft laboratory—a Frankenstein's eyes were snapping open.

There came a sudden discordant, frenzied clanging as 'Last Orders' were called. Demanding that drunken decisions must be made.

Subconsciously, his hands had betrayed him: the key now slotted in the lock. There was still blood on his hands. He battened down the hatches with last-ditch denial.

He still had options! Drop the box at the police station and be done with it.

His mother's insistent pleas receding: "You're not him, you're nothing like him!"

Like an automaton, he twisted the key. Pried open the lid, and looked ambivalently upon his past insurance; his present inheritance. Fidgeting uncomfortably; buckling under familiar yet foreign urges of a sadomasochistic 'other'. A doppelganger of his own design.

The vase was totally broken and disfigured. That dreadful potter's wheel had begun to turn. Remoulding. Restructuring. It was not grief which filled that hollow void, but like an urn from the ashes, it rose.

Periphery movement became his focus.

That pretty girl saying her goodbyes and separating from the pack.

His fingers crossed that forbidden barrier. Ignoring the assortment of polaroid trophies. He took what he needed. The restraints; the vial; the rag; the blade. Rose from his seat a transformed and determined man. The apple of his father's eye. With history rewritten.

The pretty girl turned into the alley, battling her rebellious umbrella. A fleeting consideration weighing momentarily on her mind: had she been too harsh with that young man? A desperately awkward and nervous wreck, but beyond the heavy sadness, she had seen kindness in his eyes.

She barely heard the rush of footsteps from behind.

Or the almost animalistic growl of that ancient two-word phrase.

# BODIE, THE BUCKET LIST & THE BODY SNATCHERS

"I seen 'em again—the dead dancing with the living."

Bodie didn't react straight away. Just flicked his cigarette forwards, spinning out over the rising moon and into the night. He unscrewed the cheap whiskey, and took a generous amount before passing it over to Captain Whippits—knowing it would not come back. The rusty old Ferris wheel creaked perilously as it carried them around in the dark. The silence was not peaceful. For Bodie that fairground music would forever be playing inside his head, always off-key. Whippits, he was sure, suffered too: his own inner demons pulling at whatever chords remained intact within that pickled brain. Their pod had reached its cycle's peak, with the town of Crylow Cove an overshadowed labyrinth laid out below, when Bodie finally spoke.

"Sounds like Sheriff's business."

Captain Whippits' bloodshot eyes jumped wildly around their sockets, his head shaking fiercely against that suggestion. Bodie understood. Both men had tangled with Sheriff McCarthy on numerous occasions. Both had learnt to keep their distance from that man, with little love lost between them.

Still, something troubled Bodie: a strangeness to that old clown's mad ramblings. He regarded Whippits intently as the wheel continued its descent. Bodie had heard enough of his hallucinations over the years, yet this was different. An odd logic appeared to be lurking inside the insanity. There were no new intricacies or additions to his tale. No feverish revelations, or excitedly imaginative leaps. It was this banality, the very lack of anything noticeable that had caught his attention. Bodie looked past the nervous ticks, the sleep-deprived sunken eyes, the week-old tear stains still visible through the cracked and flaking makeup. He saw truth hidden within that lunatic's confession.

Captain Whippits had thought the ride was over. Was surprised when Bodie's hands refused to let the safety bar budge an inch. His eyes sparkled upon seeing another half bottle produced as if by magic from the fairground owner's coat lining. Ascending towards the stars once more, Bodie leaned in closer, his white teeth gleaming through the darkness.

"Tell me everything you saw!"

The following day a storm rolled in off the sea, turning the world grey and the narrow roads muddy. Bodie found his father's ideology still haunting him from beyond the grave. 'Interest's an investment,' he had always warned.

"True Pa," Bodie sighed while taking refuge from the rain in O'Malley's Tavern. He had already made one 'charitable donation' in exchange for information and knew it probably wouldn't be the last. Like in so many backwater towns, the prime currency was secrets, not the dollar. Crylow Cove traded in every type of nefarious affair. Knowledge equalled power, and if meddling in other people's business was the townsfolk jonesing for a fix, then Bodie was their dealer.

The payment had been worthwhile, the grave-keeper divulging more than what would reach legal reports or newspaper pages. Four graves had been 'disturbed' within the last year. The first two were kept quiet on Sheriff McCarthy's insistence, while he launched a covert investigation. The third happened less than a month ago, and yes, true to Captain Whippits' account, the last one only two nights ago. He gave Bodie a list of the deceased whose corpses had been taken, but more importantly, offered his professional opinion as to potential motives for such an unholy crime spree.

"With one—perhaps a prank: sick kids looking for a kick," he had said. "But this? No, this had design. The night after burial, that's when they struck. Clever, you see? While the earth's still soft, and the bodies still fresh. Mark my words, whatever their reason, they wanted those corpses fresh! That leaves, I believe, three possibilities. One: they're being sold for medical research. Two: they're being used in demonic rituals by the cult that locals prefer to kid themselves no longer exists. Three: some twisted individual's using them for their own necrophiliac pleasure. My biggest fear, whichever it might be—it's clearly escalating!"

Bodie scanned the list of names again. He recognised them all—it being a small town—but research would be needed to discover any connection between them. Considering those three options, it wasn't hard for him to reshuffle them into his own private preferential order. Illegal research equalled scandal, which of course meant money, lots of it. Blackmailing some demented pervert could be lucrative too, assuming the necro-freak had money of course. Few in Crylow Cove did these days, but Bodie felt confident that such deviant habits could surely be an extravagance of the wealthy. He began thinking of hopeful suspects. The Mayor was top of his list.

The least attractive prospect was that damned cult. Supposedly eradicated some eighty years ago. Yet the rumours still lived on, rippling through the community by both the God-fearing and superstitious, hushed whisperings of bad omens from backward tongues. The last thing Bodie wanted was to get tangled up with that Satanic group. Nothing concrete had been established: their names, numbers, power and—most importantly—wealth, remained a mystery. Another of his father's sayings echoed through his mind: 'If you're gonna make someone else's business your own, better make it worth your while.'

Out the window he spotted Sheriff McCarthy, his head hung low and flowers in one hand, heading for the cemetery. Bodie cursed under his breath. Their relationship was a complicated matter: decades of competitiveness, and mostly resentment on Bodie's part. They had grown up together, had once been childhood friends, yet life—as it so often does—had indifferently sorted the wheat from the chaff. Until three years ago it had seemed that McCarthy was born under a lucky star. Opportunity and success came readily to him. That was until the Sheriff's dream world had come tumbling down. His wife, Ellen, had fallen sick: had been diagnosed with paralytic Poliomyelitis. A crippling, awful way to go and the closest Bodie had ever got to feeling pity for the man. Town gossip prevented any outward sympathy surfacing though, for even on that most morbid of topics, the Sheriff still came out smelling of roses. 'Extraordinarily caring', and a 'true romantic', just a couple of the conclusions drawn by the locals to describe a man doing everything he could to grant the last wishes of his dying wife. Ellen had always dreamed of running an ice cream parlour, you see. So McCarthy had simply bought the property adjacent to the Police Station, spent months renovating it to fulfil his wife's desires.

A goddamn ice cream parlour! Only Bodie—it appeared—had thought to question how? How, on a local Sheriff's salary could such a thing be possible? No. He had never trusted that man. Corrupt as they come, he was sure of it.

The parlour had only stayed open a month, before hobbling around it became too much for poor Ellen. 'But, at the very least,' the townsfolk had sighed, 'she got the chance to live out her dream. Even if it was only for a short while.'

Even in mourning, the Sheriff had been a disappointment. Had hit the bottle hard at first—almost lost his job on account of it—but had somehow managed to claw his way back to sobriety, regaining the respect of the people. He had kept the parlour, never opening it for business, but many suspected holding onto it as a reminder, a perfect memorial to the love that he had lost.

Bodie finished his drink and headed for the payphone.

"Danny? Is that you?"

An unmistakable grunt of confirmation.

"Got a job for you tonight, if you ain't busy."

Another grunt.

"Be outside yours at nine, and bring your tools."

Bodie had used many youngsters over the years, but young Dan Jackson had shown real promise. Seventeen: that ripe age when the future is only the adventure of the present moment and consequences a dull and distant afterthought. Danny saw a world of conspiracies, imagined himself some lone vigilante or Jason Bourne figure. He was fearless too and had proved his salt the few times when he had been caught: a tight-lipped martyr to whatever cause, refusing to talk and never once dropping Bodie's name. In many ways like a perfect sort of son. Obedient, loyal, and only costing Bodie money when he was useful.

As Bodie headed for the library, he noticed the Sheriff in

the distance, head still hanging down, hands now empty. Although their two investigations might very well run parallel, Bodie would make every effort to give that crooked lawman the widest of berths.

The two of them walked in silence, crossing the river and leaving the waterlogged town's steaming streetlights far behind them. They stood at the fork in the road for a while, their eyes picking out the distant dark chimneys and spires of the Oakdale asylum. Long enough for Danny to realise some part of that sprawling estate was to be his focus for the evening. They turned right, following a dirt track which cut through the forest, while Bodie carefully went through detailed instructions with his eager young apprentice.

"You sure you got it?" Bodie insisted, handing over the video camera along with a backup memory card.

"Abandoned sections, old morgue, any evidence of recent activity, paperwork—record and document everything." Danny repeated parrot-fashion while fixing his balaclava in place.

"Good kid!" Bodie smiled encouragingly, suppressing the sense of uneasiness which had been growing in the back of his mind. They were standing in the doorway of the junkyard's former office cabin, the low moon producing more shadows than light. "I'll be waiting for you here, and remember—"

"Don't get caught, guard up and never talk!" Danny recited the motto wearily like it was the Lord's Prayer at Sunday School.

Bodie watched him dart off through the trees, his flickering head torch beam soon disappearing from view. Bodie sighed and bit his lip nervously, unable to shake the feeling that something was wrong. Those surrounding woods still troubled him. A dreamlike memory long denied, of that horned beast he couldn't have encountered. The harrowing prophecies it had whispered, echoing and ringing like tinnitus evermore—the very reason he sought refuge within that mind-numbing fairground music.

The inside of the cabin was dank and dark, smelling of a decade's old stewing pot of piss and rot, but he gladly gave up fresh air for the comfort of being behind a closed door. The lock was busted. He considered dragging a filing cabinet over to block it, but then, what sort of message would that send his protégé when he returned. Bodie sat uncomfortably in the dark, sipping warm whiskey, his eyes never shifting from that door.

By two in the morning, he began to worry. By three, the restlessness and pacing commenced.

"Kid shoulda been back by now!" he muttered to himself.

Half an hour crawled intolerably by until a sharp and dreadful sound broke the bleakness of the silent night. It was a scream. Long, drawn-out and choking. Fading to an echo like a meteor across the sky. Bodie's agitated brain curdled with ghastly possibilities. It had been human. There was no denying that. Bodie convinced himself it had been a woman. At that pitch, no man alive would have admitted ownership of that cry.

"No! Couldn't have been—not the kid!"

Ten minutes later, another noise. The sound of shuffling outside. Faint as the tentative tread of some forest creature. Silence followed. Then a tremendous bang. A slamming at that unlocked door. The frame itself shook. The door creaked open barely an inch and stuck. Exposing just a sliver of the absolute darkness beyond. Bodie drew the hunting knife. His eyes fixed upon that crack.

Once the blackness mellowed—lightening slightly to the

deepest of blues—long before the sun had even broached the horizon, Bodie was pushing that rusted door open. He saw the video camera first, placed upon the cabin porch just outside the door. Around it, crude markings were painted: a circle of meaningless symbols. The camera seemed undamaged, and Bodie hastily checked the memory card slot: empty. A swirling pre-dawn mist carpeted the junkyard, and yet Bodie saw no movement or signs of life. The sound from behind, of the cabin door banging shut, startled him. He knew it was just the wind but, turning anxiously around, what he saw raised within his throat a fear that could not be swallowed, nor spoken. Nailed to the outside of the office door the barely recognisable remains of a dead cat. With eyes bulging and its jaw having been broken backwards, the animal had been savagely gutted, with its entrails dangling almost to the floor, swaying gently like some divining pendulum. Bodie recognised the inverted pentagram, daubed in clotted crimson streaks, encircling the body. He ran from that appalling place, never looking back nor pausing until he was safely locked inside his fairground trailer.

The morning was spent alternating between poisons, coffee and whiskey finally steadying his nerves. Bodie waited by the phone. He knew that one way or another information would come to him. News seldom stayed buried in Crylow Cove for long. Just before midday, he got the call. One of the orderlies from the hospital, who had been for over five years on his payroll.

"Dan Jackson's been brought in this morning, thought you'd wanna know. They found him out on the old tree stump up by Devil's Gate."

"What the hell was he doing there?"

"Nobody knows Bodie."

"Well, what's he been saying, dammit?"

Something unspeakable lurked within the subsequent silence. "He, he ain't said nothing. Isn't gonna be talking anytime soon, Bodie. Somebody don't want him to... made a real mess o' him!"

Bodie ground his teeth as he listened to the reported injuries: eyes burnt out, tongue severed, demonic markings carved all over the body. Strangest of all, X-rays had revealed two small, rectangular foreign objects inside the boy's stomach. The doctors weren't hopeful, and the Sheriff was on the warpath. Bodie hung up the phone, burying his head in his hands. All he could hear was the sound of rats gnawing away under the trailer, and that fairground tune playing without rhythm. Slowly his guilt transformed into anger.

By the time Sheriff McCarthy arrived to question him, Bodie had concluded that he wasn't a priority 'person of interest'. Just a formality. They danced expertly through the motions, neither divulging the information they both possessed. As the Sheriff was turning to leave, he noticed the camera which had been left out on the countertop.

"New hobby?"

"An investment!" Bodie grinned, stretching his arms out wide. "For the grand new opening, all about advertising these days!"

The Sheriff nodded gravely, fixing his hat before exiting the trailer.

"Good luck with that, Bodie."

He watched through the stained curtains until the Sheriff's car had pulled away, before returning to his work. By sundown, his eyes were sore from reading, his temples throbbed from lack of sleep. Bodie climbed the old Ferris wheel, as was his habit, to smoke and drink his way towards some form of clarity.

Nothing made sense. Even with all the articles he had printed from the library, he still couldn't find a connection between the stolen bodies. Perhaps there wasn't one? A crime of opportunity certainly fitted the necro-freak theory.

"But, both men and women…?" he thought rather innocently to himself as the pod rocked back and forth, before checking that ridiculous logic, "...if he's doing the corpses, I guess bisexuality's the least of his worries!"

Yet none of that fitted with the previous night. With what happened to Danny. Had he been caught inside the asylum, or ambushed while returning through the woods? What had he seen to warrant being left speechless and sightless? What secrets necessitated such ruthless silence? It didn't add up, and why take him all the way out to Devil's Gate? Bodie pondered the problem with more whiskey. 'It's a conspiracy!' Danny would have insisted, 'the psychologists, the cult—hell—the whole damn town's in on it!'

Bodie remained unconvinced and far from satisfied.

"Unless, deliberate misdirection..." he whispered, weighing the idea over in his head.

Danny stumbled upon something big, and to draw attention away they dragged him off to the old gorge, diced him up to make it look like some sadistic cult sacrifice. Why leave the empty camera outside the office though? Perhaps as a warning?

Immediately Bodie glanced all around the darkened fairground. Was it possible they knew who he was? That he had been the brains behind the break-in last night?

As if to answer his escalating paranoia, Bodie's gaze fell upon four individuals standing motionless over by the entrance fence. All ominously silhouetted by the dim street light behind them, with no distinguishing features discernible from that distance. His startled mind fabricated wild answers: the four corpses come to haunt him, demanding justice.

At that moment, the breeze stirred: an eerie chanting riding its invisible currents. Bodie swivelled in his seat, noticing flames along the rear perimeter fence. He counted over twenty people. A hooded mob brandishing torches, repeating that awful chorus in unison. Stuck in the quicksands of indecision, he thought of standing up and hollering, fleeing, hiding. Of unlocking his old shotgun from within the trailer cupboard: he alone knew it no longer fired. Bodie even considered dialling Sheriff McCarthy.

Suddenly the chanting stopped, and the torches disappeared. Nothing now but the barren outskirts of the town lying beyond that border fence. The night air felt pregnant with some sort of grim and static expectancy. An impalpable terror solidifying, and slowly taking form.

An impossible sound followed. That whirring motor of the Ferris wheel rattling into life. Bodie panicked, checking his pockets. Momentary relief as his fingers found it: the only starter key. Although that changed nothing. The wheel was moving on its own. Denial was futile: it was dragging Bodie down. Upon reaching the lower platform, the possessed contraption stopped: his pod rocking noisily back and forth. The fairground was empty. Still, those four ghostly figures waited by the main gate. Bodie's fear morphed into fake courage, the fragile, nihilistic type which the doomed so often share. He rose shakily from his seat, stepped off the hazardous ride and walked towards them. Approaching the rusted bars, he paused, thankful not to be facing phantoms yet still unsettled, despite recognising those four individuals. The living—more often than the dead—have an uncanny way of getting under one's skin. Bodie's bewilderment grew into suspicion. For it was a peculiar and powerful group assembled before him, one with no logical business to be standing at his gate.

He had no clue what the Mayor, the chief surgeon, the local

priest and that foreign shrink were doing there. Sounded like the start of a bad joke. They said nothing. Positioned, still as scarecrows, their faces gravely set, their eyes somehow staring right through him. That thirty-second standoff ended quite abruptly with all four slowly shaking their wealthy heads disapprovingly at him, before walking away into the shadows. Bodie understood the message, silent threats had a way of resonating the loudest.

"It is a goddamn conspiracy, Danny!"

Then another noise, now coming from behind him. This time, Bodie realised with sickening fright, from inside the fairground itself. He knew that sound all too well: the mesh screen door of his trailer slamming shut. Bodie crept towards it, gripping his hunting knife tightly. From the corner of his eye, he caught movement, a tall, dark figure running towards the port exit. He gave chase, with that demented fairground music now sped up and blaring maniacally through his brain.

Bodie knew the area well. Stalked his prey silently beyond the fences, down towards the pier with its adjacent little marina. Although he had lost sight of the intruder, Bodie remained calm, edging his way further into that dead-end quarter, confident he had the guy cornered. The marina was deserted, just battered old fishing vessels which had seen better days, all except one: Sheriff McCarthy's private yacht. Bodie sneered, spitting in contempt. Yet another extravagant and impossible purchase only last year. A sign—some folks said—of a mid-life crisis. More evidence of corruption Bodie concluded bitterly.

"One day!" Bodie whispered, mentally adding a boat to his ever-growing bucket list of pipe dream possessions.

He continued, stepping out onto the pier itself. Listening for any telltale sounds. Only the rhythmic lapping of water, slapping up against the slimy timber beams, and ancient boat ropes aching with the tide.

Then a definite tap, tap, tapping. A nearby hollow echo, disorientating and difficult to place. Bodie whirled around, seeing nothing. Then a split-second sound of rushing footsteps, the whistling of air being violently displaced, followed by a seismic crack upon the back of his skull. Blinding darkness, a sense of falling, the clatter of something being dropped, the dull thud of his limp body finally landing.

Pain brought him back to reality, consciousness returning with a vicious sting. A black cat was sitting close by, watching him with superior apathy. Bodie didn't trust cats, especially this infamous one of local legend. The Augury Cat, who had a longstanding habit of appearing only as a harbinger of imminent death.

"I ain't done for yet!" Bodie said. The cat glared back.

"Son of a—" he groaned, picking up the bloodstained object that had struck him. It was a walking cane whose sturdy, bulbous handle was engraved with intricate designs. "Probably imprinted on the back of ya bloody head," he grumbled, gingerly touching the sore spot where a lump had already formed. He recognised that walking stick from somewhere, but couldn't think where. He kept it though, used it for support to slowly hobble his way home.

The following day shook Crylow Cove to its core. Beatrice Finch, a middle-aged local woman, had disappeared on her way to work. News had spread quickly through the community. Growing panic circulating that not just the dead, but the living too were being targeted by the unknown maniac in their midst. Trust evaporated. Lifelong friends kept a cautious distance, passing one another as strangers. Thankfully for Bodie, money still talked, and his investigation continued in earnest.

Whoever had assaulted him, had also stolen the video camera from his trailer, although that could easily be replaced. He made several more payments for lesser-known information about those four respected pillars of the community. 'Living's a dirty business!' his father had used to say, and if there was dirt, Bodie was determined to find it. He was convinced that the missing corpses, poor Danny's fate, and the recent kidnapping were all connected somehow. Just the tip of the iceberg, traces of some broader, far-reaching conspiracy.

He visited the hospital. Saw all the tubes and machines keeping him barely breathing. Clean white bandages hiding all the horrific injuries. Bodie even swung by the old thrift store, coaxing information about that walking cane from the eccentric owner. "It's cursed!" had been Mrs Adelman's final judgement, but then again, being the town's 'psychic in residence' Mrs Adelman believed a great many things were cursed.

It was back inside the fairground trailer at sunset that the rush of revelatory dominos began to fall. Having accidentally spilt whiskey across the table, as he wiped up the mess of sodden papers, Bodie's eyes fell upon an old newspaper photograph he had printed from the library two days before. The article was mentioning some local fundraiser event some years back. Seven smiling faces posing side by side, and there in the middle, gripped tightly by a frail hand: that same walking cane. Seeing it, the memory came flooding back. It had belonged to the Sheriff's late wife. Bodie finished the remaining whiskey, then hurriedly threw a few things into a large bag, before racing out the door.

Two hours later, he was soaked in sweat and working the shovel furiously, already waist-deep inside the grave.

"It's just a hole, Pa!" he muttered defensively.

'And you're just digging yourself in deeper!' came his dead father's predictable response.

The chain of events which led him to this point had flashed by so quickly that Bodie hadn't had enough time to think any decision through properly. The mortician had remembered the funeral well. Had sworn blindly that Ellen McCarthy had been buried along with her walking cane. Even remembered the comment he had made to the Sheriff—in a hopeless attempt of consolation—that 'she wouldn't be needing that where she was going.'

Bodie's endeavour to convince the grave-keeper to carry out the task had failed. It became apparent that no amount of whiskey in the world would get him to illegally exhume a body. His silence and his shovel were only to be bought at a painfully high price. 'Doesn't matter,' Bodie kept telling himself afterwards, confident that the secret he was uncovering would be well worth it. Obsession was clouding his judgement. He didn't even consider how it would look if he were caught right then, in light of recent events and the general hysteria that had consumed Crylow Cove.

The sound of the shovel striking the coffin was exhilarating. Bodie frantically cleared the loose dirt and pried the lid open with his bare hands. It was just as he had suspected, although not entirely. Neither cane nor decomposing body lay inside. Instead, what filled the casket was a large quantity of what looked like thick police files, along with several evidence bags. Bodie rummaged through it eagerly, his flashlight moving over every inch of that buried coffin.

"I need to speak with Sheriff McCarthy!" Bodie demanded breathlessly.

The officer regarded him with instinctive distrust, he knew all about Bodie's past record.

"Already left. Won't be back until morning." was his firm and final reply.

Bodie left the station and stood outside considering his options. He didn't yet have proof of the suspected mass conspiracy, but whatever was going on, the Sheriff was involved. In it up to his corrupt eyeballs. As he smiled at the idea of finally taking McCarthy down, he saw the ice cream parlour next door and noticed the light was on, the front door ajar.

Bodie peered cautiously inside, but the place appeared empty. He tiptoed along the counter, examining what lay upon it. A single sheet of paper weighed down by the Sheriff's badge. 'A resignation letter?' he hypothesised, reaching over to pick it up.

It took some time to realise exactly what he was reading. It was a fairly lengthy list—not the kind for grocery shopping—but mysteriously odd in its randomness. Each line was numbered and ticked accordingly. Bodie hesitated after reading number 9: 'Own a quaint little ice cream parlour.'

Suddenly he heard a door closing at the rear of the property, soon followed by tyres screeching away at speed. Still grasping the piece of paper, Bodie hurried towards the back storeroom, desperately trying to figure out what the hell was going on. He fumbled around in the dark for the light switch.

Upon finding it, he saw the line of long, rectangular freezers, all humming steadily away. He approached the first one apprehensively and raised the lid. It was empty. Methodically he opened them all: nothing. Although, in the bottom corner of the last one, something caught his eye. Reaching in, he grasped it, tearing it away from the icy interior. He turned it over between his fingers. Human hair. Bodie could almost hear the tap, tap, tapping of the puzzle pieces clicking into place.

His eyes continued scanning the list, his heartbeat a pounding crescendo. One item was not ticked. Number 14 instead had been repeatedly circled in pen: 'A proper pleasure cruise, just us and the gang,' followed by a list of people's names. Bodie froze. Then fished out the newspaper photograph from his bag, and read the names of those seven people printed beneath it.

They all matched: the disturbed graves, the Sheriff and his wife, even poor missing Beatrice Finch. 'The gang' had all been gathered.

"This ain't part of the conspiracy!" Bodie groaned with sinking realisation. "Oh, God—I got it wrong, Pa!"

The wind howled as he ran back across those deserted, crooked, dark and narrow streets. Past the fairground fence, and heading as fast as he could towards the docks. Bodie raced along the ancient pier as the full moon appeared out from behind black clouds. Catching his breath, he spotted the Sheriff's boat leaving that small marina, silently venturing out into the vast expanse of a glittering lonely ocean. The moonlight bathed it magical: a breathtaking scene, an endless glossy and rippling canvas of oil and snow.

Bodie could clearly see six figures all seated on board and in a circle. Only one of them was thrashing violently around. Beatrice Finch must have been bound and gagged, but Bodie believed he could just make out her muffled screams. Most likely terrified by those familiar old faces; the frozen company she was currently being forced to keep. At the helm stood Sheriff McCarthy. For the first time, Bodie truly understood. Saw him as nothing more than a broken man fulfilling a final promise.

Shaking his head, Bodie turned away, that off-key fairground tune still playing—a little more tragically now—through his mind. He hadn't gone more than a dozen paces before that same black cat appeared. It crossed his path further ahead, before stopping and watching him approach.

As Bodie drew near, he paused, turning back to glance at the boat now drifting in the distance. Seconds later, a single gunshot rang out across the quiet water. Bodie hung his head low for a few moments before lifting it once more. The cat was still staring. Bodie stared straight back. It had been a strange few days, even by the rather disturbing standards of a town like Crylow Cove.

"So, imminent death, huh?" he pondered out loud. The tip of the cat's tail flicked keenly back and forth. "I've got a rat problem at the fairground if you wanna earn your keep?"

Its bright eyes flashed back at him through the darkness. A devilish purr of anticipation rising. Bodie shifted the weight of the large bag to his other shoulder. Stuffed full with all those secret files and evidence bags from the grave.

"Nothing stays buried forever!" Bodie said sagely, borrowing yet another of his father's mottos. The Augury Cat appeared unimpressed, but stayed close to Bodie's heels. The two of them sauntering off, side by side through a night which both of them believed they owned, and heading home.

# ORGANIC DEFENCES

*FOR "THE LIGHT"*

She was born during the great freeze. Born with the heart of an adventurer, but the physicality of a dewdrop. As she grew, so did her uncertainties. For the world seemed far too small, too neatly presented and efficient to be true. Life was terminally cloistered and linear, without the possibility of parole, and yet she found herself yearning for something more, something unknown. She had studied hard, and learnt to work with a kind of outward obedience—a carefully fitted mask—which belied her ever budding resentment and longing for adventure.

During her adolescence came the first signals of a possible, creeping thaw. She remembered a sense of excitement and hope had flourished within the community back then: but that all seemed so very long ago now. A rapid and endless flurry of building had followed, matched only by a focus on the necessary procedures to protect the citadel. Conscription, as a concept, was nothing new to her and had not come as any great surprise: it was the yoke of social inclusion after all, and so it came to pass that she was posted to The Wall.

The Wall had been there forever, perfectly impenetrable and enclosing the commonwealth for the greater common good.

Although the nameless, God-like architect had left no clear instructions, one look through that blurry translucent barrier was enough to convince the collective conscience. Beyond its layer of protection lay a grotesquely psychotropic world. Terrifying creatures of dark and diabolical proportion slithered and swarmed upon the other side. It was the quintessential stuff of nightmares: beings so foreign and unfamiliar that there could be no hope of any union or concord. The age-old motto of her tribe was as simple as it was inflexible: 'Keep the invaders out at any cost.'

She never told anyone what she had witnessed, just before the end of her previous shift. Had done her best to deny and suppress the memory, but still, she found it weighing heavily on her mind.

She couldn't be certain of what she had seen, for the truth was that the encounter had been as fleeting as it was wondrous in nature. The Wall had filtered the whole experience into obscurity and doubt, but some wayward part of her was so very desperate to believe.

Like a vision, the being had approached the outer side of The Wall. At first, it had appeared dark and alien, just as all those other sinister monstrosities out there, and yet it did not move in quite the same manner. It had hovered gracefully as it drew near, as though contemplating the divisive barrier, before turning its full attention towards … her. She, in turn, had for some unfathomable reason stepped closer and committed the cardinal sin of pressing one palm up against that supple membranous film. There was intelligence in the creature's large, almond-shaped eyes. No, not just intelligence, but something else: kindness.

To even consider such a thing would be judged by the community as blasphemous, so she kept quiet. Her heart, however, would not be silenced. With every flash of visual recall, she became more and more convinced that she had seen an angel. Those delicate and wide silhouetted wings which moved at such distorted speeds as to appear static: they had held the impossibility of actually possessing colour. The longer she thought about this, the more dubious the brickwork of their social doctrines, their inherited assumptions of knowledge had seemed.

The question that arose consumed her: what if it was The Wall itself that was misrepresenting the outside world, diffusing all colour and beauty and twisting everything that lay beyond into a dark and ominous black. She had shuddered, barely daring to even think where such a logical prospect might lead: What if The Wall itself could not be trusted?

The time for deliberation and internal wrestling had passed; her decision had been made. Her mind was aching as she stood there, on the cusp of reality and all that she knew. Behind her, the familiar bustle of the colony building, growing, furiously stretching itself towards bursting point. She never once looked back. Now was the time for courage, and she took one more determined step right up to the glistening red surface of The Wall.

"They probably won't even realise that you've gone," she told herself quietly, knowing the statement was false, but hoping it would sound more reassuring than it did. Pressing both her hands against its surface, she began to force herself forward with all the strength that she possessed. There came the faintest sound of tearing, but she did not stop. She squirmed and pushed onwards towards the promise of freedom. Out of that tight womb-like prison—the world that had been her cocoon—she slid, emerging sticky in the sweltering silent heat, and tumbled down the outer side of The Wall, blinded by the dazzling blue.

Under the impassive glare of the mid-morning sun, the ants were the first insects to attack that small tear, where the ripened skin had split. They were not to be the last and paid very little attention to the tiny trickle of juice which had burst out of the opening, rolling exquisitely with the first kiss of gravity, as the tomato wept.

# WORLD OF SHADOWS

At exactly 09:47, Thursday, March 16th 2017, I thought I must have gone insane. Now, one week later, I have been told that today, at sunset—I shall no longer exist here. Consider these pages my final testimony, while I am still of this world.

Seven days of peculiar captivity have allowed me plenty of time for reflection and thought. A way to unravel the subtle tapestry which I once, so proudly and possessively, considered my life. It was the beginning of September last year when all of this began. Naturally, I was oblivious: how is a person to realise that he is being targeted for something which has not yet come to pass?

Many would have described my situation as 'tragic' at that time, but perhaps a brief elucidation might go some way to help you understand my current state of mind. In quick succession, I had been tag-teamed and betrayed by life and then death. My wife leaving me for another man left me numb, but then, as a loyal friend later reasoned: to put your faith in an actress is like storing water in a sieve. Their profession is to lie convincingly for a living, so you shouldn't be shocked to find yourself part of their performance. This loss was closely followed by the news that the grandmother who had raised me had passed away quite unexpectedly. The sum of those two events had left me utterly hollow and in an emotionally vegetative state.

Her Executor was to be the unlikely person who would rouse me from the inertia of depression. That my grandmother had left me everything came as little surprise since there was nobody else, but through whatever reason or fancy, she had booked me a cabin on a luxury cruise ship.

So it was that on January 10th, I embarked at Southampton for a round-the-world trip which was meant to last one hundred days. Little did I know then that I was the only passenger destined not to return in late April.

What occurred just before boarding that vessel was—in hindsight—an early warning sign missed. My far from gregarious existence on various social media platforms was the first strategic move played against me. I rationalised it as best I could. Divorce and grief can often stir unappealing and leper-like visions in others, with many choosing to keep their distance. So it happened that, on New Year's Day, I watched the steady disappearance of both friends and followers. The thought did cross my mind that those accounts had been hacked but, with this grand adventure looming, I preferred to focus on other things.

Only now am I beginning to understand their intent. Had they wanted to stop me, they could have easily gone for my bank accounts, my passport. No. By reasoning and logic, I have concluded: they wanted me on that boat!

For all the wondrous sights and exotic ports, my real voyage of discovery arose unscheduled. Two nights after we had set sail from Fremantle, Australia, headed for Mauritius, at well past midnight, I decided to take a stroll on deck, despite the inclement weather. One moment I was being buffeted along those rails. Whether I climbed, lost my balance, or was lifted and pushed over by the gale: those possibilities seem irrelevant now. The howling ferocity ceased, replaced by a muted gurgling rush, bordering almost on silence. Spluttering I resurfaced, with the cold realisation that I—without any likely witness to raise the alarm—had fallen overboard. In that eternal, rolling darkness, I almost surrendered. The easiest thing, to simply stop kicking.

The dawn arrived with a horrendous fusion of hope and despair. An empty ocean, whose enormous rising swells offered nothing to my desperate eyes. To the west, a low stormcloud, creeping ever closer, its shimmering darkness and heavy rains churning the waters into misty clouds of grey. At 08:35, I realised the storm was in fact not heading my way, but instead that I was drifting towards it. Soon after that, I briefly entertained the delusion that just maybe I would pass it by.

By 09:32, with the torrential rain falling in sheets, less than a few hundred metres away, I resigned myself to a watery grave. With regular lightning flashes illuminating that otherwise menacing sky, the only question was whether I would even be allowed the opportunity to drown. A few minutes later, another terrifying possibility presented itself, adding to my overall hysteria: the unmistakable sensation of something large brushing up against my lower leg. Instinctively and against my best efforts, the music from Jaws burrowed its way into my brain.

My panic was so intense, floating into that raging downpour, that I heard no gentle lapping. Something else struck my upper thigh. I closed my eyes and prayed for electrocution. Those predators beneath the surface seemed to swarm in unison, going in for the kill. I remember thrashing about wildly, stealing one last lungful of air, before pausing in sudden bewilderment.

Unsteadily, I rose to my knees, grasping around frantically

until I was quite sure it was solid rock beneath me. Then the struggle to haul myself up and out of the water. I cowered there shivering and, looking down, saw that the ground upon which I stood was not visible. Totally transparent, with only the waves seemingly still passing violently underfoot some several feet below.

That was at 09:47.

Walking on air—I found—was quite a tricky business. I staggered onward through the driving wind and rain until I passed through what I can only attempt—and fail—to describe as some sort of thick, semi-solid film or membrane.

The land beyond that barrier was vast and strange. As I marvelled at the surrounding greenery, the inexplicably clear blue skies, I quickly became convinced of a rather disturbing fact: that I was not the first person to step foot upon that island. For the few hours which followed, nothing made much sense.

My rough estimation was that I was perhaps one thousand miles off the west coast of Australia. Yet to my geographic recollection, no landmass of such size existed there. I followed what was once perhaps a well-trodden path, observing occasional bits of debris, remnant signs of human life along the way.

By midday, I reached a deserted settlement of sorts. Crude and basic, with a line of primitive-looking huts positioned in a semicircle. At the centre of that clearing, a large fire pit, but what had been erected, twenty yards further away, appeared to defy all explanation.

It was an empty rectangular frame, standing vertically at around twelve feet tall, and eight feet wide. There was an intricacy to its design, an advanced look to it, quite out of place somehow. I examined it closely: a metallic construct, the colour of lead. I ran my fingers over it, walked around it, even stepped right through it, but nothing. After that, I turned my attention to those abandoned huts, and from within their musty insides, not answers but, scraps of information were retrieved.

From the materials and makeshift furniture, it appeared the majority of those absent inhabitants had arrived by sea. There was a noticeable nautical decor, most likely salvaged from shipwrecked vessels. In one of the huts, I found an exception: three individual seats in very terrible condition, but easily recognisable as those which would typically be found upon a modern passenger plane. Nothing within those dwellings suggested a historical timeline stretching back much beyond the last fifty years. The visible signs of disrepair and dust led me to believe that the place had been vacant for some time, perhaps years. 'Maybe they were rescued?' I considered hopefully to myself.

On an improvised writing desk, made from wooden crates, I discovered a small notebook, almost completely filled, upon whose final pages I write this letter now. The previous owner's handwriting was awful and, feeling exhausted and unsure what else to do, I sat outside for a few hours, attempting to decipher that scrawling penmanship.

Page after page devoted to something called the Mandela Effect which, in all honesty, sounded to me more like the unreliable functioning of the human brain—which we know precious little about—and its ability to recreate false memories. The supposed 'proof' of this wild theory was tenuous at best.

Miniscule changes to the past, hardly seeming worthy reasons for justifying time travel. That was until it discussed the subject of the movement and disappearance of individual islands. More relevantly one located to the west of Australia and, in true conspiracy-nut fashion, coinciding with one of the supposed search areas for the recently missing Malaysia Flight MH370.

Under ordinary circumstances, I would have dismissed its

contents as the work of a lunatic, drunk on seawater. Although, since that day, I have read every fantastically absurd page several times. That afternoon, however, I was interrupted without warning, and most unpredictably.

A slight periphery movement caught my attention. Looking up, I froze in fear, paralysed by the chimerical impossibility of what I was seeing. Maybe it's the lifelong sceptic in me, but if one is forced to endure such an encounter, one would assume it in the dead of night, not in broad daylight.

The clearing had quite literally 'come alive' with countless figures, all converging silently upon me. I think it's fair to say that my rational compass, my grip on any sense of reality, was shattered at that moment. For I was surrounded not by people, but by an army of dark shadows. That was the first, and by no means the last, visitation from these strange pioneers who had made this island their home. Though I have learned a great many truths over the last week, several questions still remain unanswered.

While the unknown author of that notebook talks endlessly about insubstantial conspiracy theories, I will attempt to keep to the facts. Yes, by their own admission, these 'shadow people' are a highly advanced race who come from the distant future. It was a great relief to my incredulous and fragile psyche when one among them—with whom I have since conversed the most—revealed to me its real form.

Within our world, they choose to move in the guise of shadows, although it would not be pressed as to explain exactly why. When the shadow positioned itself on the other side of that empty frame, its portrait became crystal clear.

I say 'it', since I could not ascertain a specific gender with any certainty. Their appearance is almost human, noticeably more slender and graceful, with delicately elfin features, and larger eyes.

They arrived in the late 1940s, having chosen this particular island as their base of operations. With their superior technology, they promptly camouflaged the entire peninsula from our rudimentary scientific means of perception, before going a little further back in history to erase any record of its existence.

Their achievements—or at least those they have admitted to—are enormous. They have mastered not only time travel, but also teleportation, telepathy and inter-dimensional travel.

I firmly believe that perhaps through the passing of millennia or genetic evolution, even though our two species may be remotely related, their wisdom has made them a distinctly kinder creature. Sadly I think we could only fail to truly understand their business and intentions here, due to the very nature of our limitations. Although, the fact they have chosen our specific time and dimension suggests, at least to me, that we must be doing something catastrophically wrong.

I was fascinated to discover that they knew everything about me; had known in advance about my impending arrival, and had been the omniscient perpetrators behind my social media 'ghosting'. That—they confided—was a preliminary step in what they referred to mysteriously as the 'phasing out process'.

When I finally plucked up the courage to ask what had become of the others who had fatefully landed upon that island, I immediately wished I hadn't. My newfound friend—and I feel both proud and confident in using such a descriptive—replied that they no longer exist here. Sensing my worry and concern at hearing this, a more detailed and reassuring explanation followed swiftly.

I was told how, quite recently, an aeroplane crash had caused the shadow people a fair amount of work. What they termed as 'relocation' was apparently quite a complicated affair. Due to the clandestine nature of their work, once someone had stepped foot upon their island, the possibility of that person returning to their normal life was not an option.

It had taken almost a year before the final survivor from that crash had been successfully relocated. My case was somewhat more fortunate, as there was a 'parallel opening' forecasted within a week. These 'openings' were indeed a dizzying concept.

They referred to the moment when one of your 'other selves', co-existing within the numerous alternate universes or dimensions, was about to die. In essence, such openings were a well-timed, bodysnatcher swap-out of sorts. Taking the form of miracle recoveries from terminal illnesses, or fortuitous escapes from fatal accidents. These 'relocations', however, seldom ran smoothly. The 'imposter' doubles frequently struggled to acclimatise and fit in, to what was often a slightly unfamiliar family and world. But then—as was explained quite eloquently—it was a commonly accepted trait of primitive humans across all dimensions to act with inexplicable irrationality at times.

I have only two alternatives and have weighed them very carefully, for it is, without doubt, the most significant decision of my life. I must leave soon if I am to reach the coast and still manage to return to this clearing by the designated hour. These pages will be placed within a sealed bottle, and float wherever the waves will carry them.

My friend has made it clear to me that, were I to choose to travel through this 'parallel opening', there would be no guarantees within the selected alternate universe. My life there could be indistinguishably the same, in nearly every way. Or, I might arrive to find my grandmother alive, and an ex-wife still faithfully by my side.

Having weighed my life objectively, I have come to the conclusion that fortune has often favoured me. Would my 'other selves' have been so lucky? The truth is, enduring those recent personal tragedies all over again, or living in fear of the day that my parallel history might repeat itself, would be a life I could not survive.

The only other possibility allowed, is for me to be sent to that very same future from which these shadow people have come. In many ways—as with so many things in life—what I feared would be the hardest of choices, ended up being an incredibly simple one.

I believe I am now ready to let go, to stop treading water: clinging onto a world which, until so recently, I thought I knew. Prepared to face even an entirely unknown future with hope.

# THE CRUELEST COHABITATION

We were wedded without choice. Unwittingly I walked down that anaemic aisle with you: blind to the early warning signs of a one-way dysfunctional relationship. Like a cancer, your sickness has gradually spread. Everywhere I go, you remind me of my limitations. Bound forever to a temporal world, rotating through this 'mortal coil'. Our irreversible destiny, doomed to live and die together. You say nothing. Never apologise. Just continue to shine on silently, polluting my youthfulness in a way which I have grown to loathe.

I should have cut you out of my life long ago. Before all of your hoary friends moved in and made themselves at home.

When you first appeared all lost and alone, I felt sorry for you, overtly protective of you. I succumbed: was initially seduced by the strange way you complimented me. How, by your very presence, you made me feel special, made me seem a little more sophisticated and intelligent somehow. That time has passed.

I still have the potential for revenge, you know. I too could move like quicksilver: do something extreme and unexpected, to shake you from your dismal apathy. I could shave my hair completely, or dye it any colour of the rainbow. What would all your friends think of that? Could you even be capable of feeling embarrassment?

All romance is dead. We know one another far too well for any such foolishness to have survived. But you have gone too far this time! At the very least, I had resigned myself to the fact that ours would be an intellectual and platonic arrangement. Until two nights ago, when I found you growing uninvited and working your wicked magic down there.

Something must be done. Otherwise, you and I both know that only in death shall we part. I see you grinning smugly at that—believing that you're always one step ahead of me. Well, perhaps, I'll surprise you.

I've decided on cremation, by the way. Does that scare you?

The thought of all those flames relentlessly licking away any evidence of your touch, even the minutest trace. All our leaden, relinquished labours finally reduced to ash. Why, you ask? Well, as irrational as it might sound, I couldn't stand the nightmarish possibility of being buried with you! I've already chosen the urn. It's magnificent: perfectly auburn like my previous, natural colour.

You have left me no choice but to take drastic action. You will not see it coming. Your very memory shall be blotted out, eradicated from existence. I've been brushing up on chemicals, you see. Hydrogen Peroxide for me will be like Cyanide to you. So go on. Here: take a good last look at yourself, you heartless bastard. You and all your pasty friends. Say goodbye to your monochrome life, and our pallid reflection.

Still—undaunted by any of those threatening thoughts—the mirror's portrait remains bleak. Still, those grey hairs glitter and grow.

# BOUND BY THE GREATER GOOD

"Your shirt's ironed, and don't forget the cufflinks. I bought them, especially—for good luck."

She kissed him goodbye at the door, then sagged against it with the similar worry—she imagined—that a mother might feel, dropping her child off for the first day of school.

"I feel physically sick!"

In fairness, she thought, he did look awful: had returned looking that way.

"Darling, I'm sure most people feel the same way with a new job, first day jitters."

His eyes locked despairingly onto hers, only for a second, before he shook his head sadly. Strange laughter gurgled from his throat, the kind that suggests mental defeat and impending tears.

"Not like this," he replied sorrowfully, his head hung low.

She had lived with him for over a year, but had never seen him act this way.

With a sudden burst of nervous energy, he was pacing the room once more, ranting wild assertions to himself, of which she only caught parts.

"Should have known… totally unqualified… too good to be…."

She felt a pang of guilt watching him, after all, she had been the one who had encouraged and pushed him to apply for that position. His usual, cheerful confidence and unflappable composure had deserted him; only an incoherent mumbling wreck remained. He had the look of a man about to break, and it was her responsibility to pull him back away from that ledge.

"Perhaps a drive, to clear your head?" she suggested, jangling the keys. He froze; considering the idea—she hoped. No. His head shook emphatically, and the pacing resumed.

"What can I do?" she implored, before deciding to change tack. "You could always tell me what happened, what exactly it was that went wrong?"

She knew he couldn't. MI6 demanded absolute confidentiality, everything totally hush-hush: 'Semper Occultus' to the grave. Surely he remembered that. He turned now to face her with fear in his eyes, his mouth opening, but thankfully no words came out. Perhaps, she thought, the worst was over.

The next instant, he grabbed her arm and dragged her urgently into the bathroom. Panic flooded her mind as he pulled them both into the shower cubicle, firmly shut the glass door, and turned on the water. The cold was the least of her concerns as they huddled there, fully clothed beneath the powerful jet. It was the intent in his eyes: a man preparing to make a calculatedly impossible leap. He drew her close, whispering earnestly into her ear.

She closed her eyes.

"The job wasn't Data Analysis at all. The whole thing, was

a bloody lie! What they've done—what they're doing—it's insane. If I hadn't seen the proof of it with my own eyes..."

"Stop!" she pleaded, desperately wrestling to cover his mouth.

"You don't understand. They're re-writing history! Not propaganda, actual events, global bloody events!" he saw her jaw drop, her shocked expression. Knew he could not adequately explain the totality of what he had observed, but carried on regardless. "I saw the reports, the screens—entire countries completely gone!"

"That's—"

"I know, impossible right?" he pulled her even closer. "But it isn't, I've seen it! North Korea: ashes. Destroyed months ago! They're spoon-feeding people a... a more manageable, fabricated reality, and that's only the beginning.

"They've been at this for years, made a business—no, an Art of it! To pull it off, they must have people everywhere. The sheer manpower to turn fiction into credible fact... it's terrifying!" having purged those crippling secrets he collapsed, weeping bitterly and burying his head into the nape of her neck.

She needed to take control of the situation, she told herself sternly, shaking off her stunned disbelief.

"It's going to be okay," she reassured him soothingly, switching the dial to a warmer temperature. "You stay here, let me fetch you some dry clothes." He nodded, feebly trying and failing to unbutton his shirt. "No, keep them on for now." she said, stroking his cheek tenderly. "We're going to get through this," she promised, lightly kissing his forehead before exiting the shower.

A full minute passed, his brain focusing solely on staying upright—his world becoming Vertigo. Repeatedly banging his head in frustration against the tiled wall didn't restore the sense of balance, but it helped somehow.

"What have I done…" he groaned pitifully.

It was then that he noticed a sudden acrid smell: licking his lips, he found an unpleasant chemical taste to the water. Disorientation, dizziness and nausea swept over him. He tried to cry out, but couldn't. Through the steam, he saw the shadow of his girlfriend moving obliviously around the bathroom. He pounded a numb fist against the glass. She didn't appear to notice, was bent over, reaching for something within the boiler-tank cupboard. He fumbled for the shower door; succeeding only in smearing away a streak of condensation from the glass.

Through it he saw her clearly, talking gravely on her mobile phone. Probably getting the number of a psychotherapist or the nearest asylum, he considered deliriously. Nothing seemed very serious anymore.

When she turned to face him, he became puzzled. Her expression seemed distant and altogether unfamiliar. She was holding something in her left hand, some device which she pointed in his direction. He heard two hollow, mechanical clicks, and looking down saw that those lucky cufflinks had moved somehow: rotated and transformed.

"Fancy!" he slurred.

Something from within them was moving beneath his shirt cuffs, edging up his forearms. Then a tight pinch, with the smooth delicacy of papercuts. Through increasingly blurred vision, he saw what must have been blood soaking through his sleeves and pouring from the deep lacerations on either wrist. He felt no pain. Bewildered and quickly losing consciousness, through the glass, his eyes found hers. It was her head that was now shaking sadly.

# TWO WRONGS JUST MIGHT...?

The blacksmith and the veterinarian eyed one another apprehensively. At that moment, both were silently grappling with their own morality or God. The inescapable fact was that their time had come. Their worry-lines, lack of saliva and clammy sweats: all signs of the physical cracks appearing, as the psychological pressure mounted. A gentle hand resting upon one another's shoulders confirmed that they would remain united, stand firm and play out their respective parts until the very end. With deep breaths, they steadied their nerves and turned to face the line of young men.

Only yesterday, those five men had been the very picture of elegance. Jubilantly posing upon those courthouse steps, before the shutter-snap lenses of the world's media. Flashing their perfectly white and disarming smiles. No fangs or claws on show. Standing there they had shone: with a 21st Century Narcissus-like aura; boyband material; surely every parents pride and joy.

One among them had taken the questionable celebration too far: had frantically shaken and popped a foaming bottle, dousing and spraying cheap Cava liberally over his comrades.

They had laughed, they had joked. The local crowd had looked on in subdued and awkward silence. That had been yesterday, and an awful lot had happened since then.

Before them now those same five men; stripped naked and bound securely by both their wrists and ankles to that spaced-out row of chairs. The two of them, an unlikely pair of keepers, were all too well aware that the young men would be regaining consciousness soon. In a few hours, the sun would have risen, by which time their duty must have been fulfilled. Yet here, shrouded in that pre-dawn stillness, the veterinarian was struggling to suppress her doubts.

From the corner of her eye, she noticed one of their captive's heavy head loll recklessly from side to side, attempting to shake off the drugs. The blacksmith must have seen it too. With a reassuring squeeze of her shoulder, he turned, picked up his bellows and headed towards his makeshift smithy furnace. She commenced with final checks; carefully inspecting her tools and the five silver trays, each containing the exact same assortment of pre-prepared syringes. For the first time, she appreciated why—throughout history—executioners had worn masks: deeply regretting now their leader's insistence that none of the participants should do so.

"No more hiding." he had told them. "We must all own our actions!"

She knew now the finesse with which such strong, principled ideals can roll so smooth and persuasively off the tongue. A groaning slur from one of her captives snapped her back from that philosophical reflection.

Since her part was to be carried out first, the pair had agreed that—once their subjects were compos mentis—the blacksmith would be the one to provide those young men with an outline explanation of what was to come. He did so stoically, with folded arms and such a cold, inhumane matter-of-factness that his demeanour must, she was sure, have seemed terrifying. With a masked expression of indifference, she reminded herself, while he spoke, of the many occasions over the last few weeks where she had witnessed his caring, warmer natural side.

Once he was done, her medical training took over, and she began methodically to administer the anaesthetics. Her first patient had thrashed about wildly, even bitten his tongue in the process; the second had begged and pleaded; the third had merely whimpered like a little lost boy. She should have guessed from the hateful glare that the fourth—whom she now presumed their ringleader—had no intention of going under gracefully. He did not struggle or fight, but with an odious stare, spat out his final promise.

"Next time we go hunting, we're coming for you. For you and your family!"

With the needle already stuck beneath his skin, she had paused.... That second had seemed an eternity, and she found that it took every ounce of goodness in her soul to deliver him the entire recommended dose. That moment of hesitation would trouble and haunt her, now and then, for the rest of her life.

A sequence of further injections followed, and it was stern professionalism which kept her going. That cocktail of drugs, specifically chosen, to both obliterate the libido, and negate the possibility of any future sensation, or pleasure from that organ. Once over, she looked upon the pliers, and rubber elastrator rings with disdain. She had never felt entirely comfortable using such banding methods, even on smaller animals, and was glad to leave it lying there. Instead, she reached for the first scalpel.

Surgical versus chemical castration had been a tender issue. One which had sharply divided the group, and even as a veterinarian, she—at first—had taken some convincing. In the end, it had all boiled down to time and opportunity: chemical castration by itself would require continued treatments—an improbable option with all things considered. Once the mind had conquered the brutality and irreversibility of the act, it really was the only logical solution open to them.

"They're no different from animals," was the mantra she whispered under her breath throughout. Delicately and with great patience, she completed the procedures, as though on autopilot. Only when washing her hands afterwards, did her mind begin to wander. First, to the unsavoury projection of herself as a modern-day Lady Macbeth; frantically scrubbing away the bloodstains, so difficult to erase. Then she thought back over the many meetings. How, in the beginning, the group's number had grown exponentially at the simple inception of 'doing something.' A passionately naive consensus about formulating some sort of plan.

She recalled noticing the man who would eventually become the Master Architect of the movement: had initially thought very little of him. A quite strange little man. For the first two meetings, he had remained suspiciously mute, constantly scanning those assembled, with a scowl of almost pessimistic consideration. Never once seeming to pay any attention to the various people talking, instead, focusing only on the reactions of the audience. When he had finally decided to speak, his first words did very little to inspire confidence.

"I fear that many of you will have abandoned ship by the time this deed needs doing. Such is human nature."

He spoke with such a convincing air of authority that everyone had felt obliged to listen. Only later did they discover his credentials: a highly esteemed Doctor of Anthropology. He had first insisted on the importance of clarifying motive; that the group reach an honest agreement on what it was that they hoped to achieve.

"This movement must not be driven by a desire for revenge," he had warned. "Make no mistake, we will be branded as vigilantes, but unlike traditional vigilantism, we cannot consider ourselves above the law. We must take accountability for our actions. These men are not the first to commit such crimes, although their shameless intent to act outside of our socially accepted standards is what must be checked. Cause and effect. We will endeavour to reconstruct the very concept of community justice.

"I have designed a viable framework for this task which I feel could, with your willing participation, set a firm precedent for future generations. As the orchestrator, I'm committed to accepting full responsibility for the project's creation. However, all those who wish to follow through must sign a document accepting equal culpability, binding us together in shared complicity. The only other thing I need now from you is a list specifying everyone's profession. For, those wishing to stay onboard will each have an important role to play."

That was how it had all began.

She remembered him approaching her privately at a later date, once the solid plan had been discussed and settled, and after—as he had predicted—several faces had disappeared from their number. She had noticed deep concern within his steady eyes.

"Your role is regrettably severe."

She had nodded grimly.

"And you're a mother, correct?"

"I have a son and a daughter, although I'm afraid they're still too young to understand."

"A mother's instinct to protect her cubs," he had pondered

meditatively. "I'm sure your daughter will grow to understand and be proud of the sacrifice you have made for her."

"I'm not doing this for her," she had responded sharply. "A mother must also teach, and what better or more valuable precedent to set for my boy? These old ways of thinking must change."

"Very good!" the anthropologist had replied, seeming somehow reassured, and smiling warmly back at her.

Then the news had broken: early release for 'good behaviour', and some misogynistic reasoning that they were 'unlikely to re-offend.' Following the men's insultingly reduced sentences, the plan had gone smoothly, without hitch or glitch. With each individual from the group dutifully playing their part.

Their *policeman* who allowed their *journalist* to approach those five men, offering them a staggering sum—courtesy of their *property investor*—in exchange for an exclusive interview. Their local *nightclub owner* for allowing his premises as the location for the meet last night.

Their three glamorous *models*, who endured the young men's lecherous hounding, ensuring that they remained at the bar long after the interview had finished. Their *barmen* for plying the newly released convicts with the sedative-laced alcohol. Their *bouncers* for later carrying those limp, unconscious bodies to the awaiting vehicles.

Their *postman*, *taxidriver* and *ambulance crew* who all chauffeured the five to the outskirts of town. And finally, the local *farmer* in the group, for permitting his secluded barn to be used for the pair's now almost completed task.

Her thoughts were interrupted by the blacksmith, busying himself behind her. Looking down, she was pleased upon inspection to see that her hands were finally clean. She stood next to him in silence for a minute, feeling the scorching heat from the fire prickle her skin.

"We're going to Hell for this, you know that?" she said distantly.

"I've spent my life looking into the flames, searching for some kind of meaning. When the barrel's become as rotten as this, perhaps all one can do is carve out the sickness? Or at the very least mark it?" he replied, similarly hypnotised. Then snapping out of it, and with more purpose to his tone, "I'm ready." lifting the first in the row of small branding irons from the hearth.

There was a soothing symmetry between that bright metal glow and the distant sunrise, now creeping across the horizon. Some spiritual affinity with the dawn and the natural world around them.

One by one, and with great skill, the blacksmith seared the word 'Rapist' across each of the young men's foreheads. As she cleaned and bandaged those permanent scars, she spotted a line of figures walking resolutely along the dirt track towards them. Before departing, the pair unshackled the somewhat less elegant and infamously boastful Wolfpack. A group who—once the anaesthetic wore off—would awaken transformed, and crawl away to lick their wounds. Forced to face the consequences and reality of a new day; a new world; a new beginning.

The successful conspirators solemnly embraced one another outside, before linking hands in solidarity and commencing the long walk towards the police station, to confess their crime. It was as they passed through those sleepy suburbs, heading for the town centre, that the unexpected happened.

Front doors began to open: residents exiting their properties and joining the group's ranks. Many held pre-made placards with various slogans of support: 'I'm accountable too', 'We were all accomplices', and the like.

The veterinarian noticed the anthropologist smiling quietly to himself, perhaps at this other inevitability of human nature?

As their vastly increased number approached the station, none among them could have predicted the frenzy that would follow. Over the next few days, the group found solace from within their holding cells, as news of their actions reverberated around the world, going viral with a legion of supporters declaring joint responsibility, under the hashtags #IKnewToo and #MakeItRight.

# THE QUESTIONABLE CORPSE

Head groggy, vision blurred: a painful spectrum filled with glittering confetti. The consequence of too much bubbly. She ricocheted her way unsteadily through the unfamiliar rented apartment.

Re-entering the kitchen, she instantly realised nothing was the same. Cupboards laid bare—not ransacked—but with every item off the shelf, arranged neatly in rows, lining the counters like some static congregation. Dalíesque, with even the salt and pepper pots side by side, positioned ceremoniously at the forefront.

Her unflinching focus was wedded to the stranger's dead body, sprawled face-down across the kitchen table. With rising panic she called for her boyfriend: Matthew would know what to do.

Nausea and denial led her to the window. She struggled to open it, then finally breathed in the sickly scent of some distant, bitter-sweet bouquet. Her meditation was broken by an unexpected sound beside her. She turned towards the ornamental birdcage: it was no longer empty! It had been, she was sure.

It was the fashionably antique, decorative sort: prettily vacant, without any legitimate purpose. She remembered—upon their late arrival the night before—trailing her fingertips over its bars, wondering whether it was the congenial accessory her life was missing. An archetypal symbol, whose door—depending on her unconscious mood—might often remain open, other days stay closed.

Far away, a dreamlike semi-awareness of Matthew making the necessary phone-calls, announcing their current predicament and status. She preferred this less gruesome distraction: the mystery of the newly imprisoned songbird.

"Whoever she was, she must have decided this herself, must have wanted this." her boyfriend mused.

"And the Police?"

"On their way. Dealing with other engagements first." his tone inexplicably calm.

Talons rattled: the bird getting to grips with its new perch.

"We should plan our day, get on with the rest of our lives." he proposed, his indifference too surreal.

"What are you going to wear?"

"I don't care what I have to wear," she mumbled. She was beginning to doubt the very fabric of her senses. Could this nonsensical crime scene be some twisted, nightmarish Wonderland of her own mind's design?

"Suit yourself," he sighed, vanishing towards the bedroom.

The songbird began to sing a forlorn and tragic tune, each note a regret-ridden dirge to suffocated love. Suddenly she found herself drawn to the corpse as though an invisible psychic umbilical linked them both. She had to understand. Whispering a solemn vow, she reached out, grasping the matted hair, and raised that lifeless head.

"This isn't real!"

Somewhere in the distance, church bells were poignantly

ringing, for both the dead girl and the living. Cries of alarm and the frantic beating of wings behind her: a reminder that they were three within that very room. Dissociated triplets? Herself, that dead girl and the songbird? The Present, Past and Future: enmeshed metaphorically within that Twilight Zone moment. She recognised the dead girl: her former self. Saw the dazzling glint from the diamond ring wrapped ever so tightly around her own finger...

...and remembered the question, to which she had said yes.

# SERVED COLD

"Don't cry," she soothed, dabbing tenderly at the spittle and drool. Then wrapped the woollen scarf around her husband's neck, as tightly as her arthritic fingers would allow.

"It's blowing a gale out, you'll see. Better to keep warm."

She dragged him out of the cottage, manoeuvering his wheelchair along the gravel drive. Their daily routine defensible on 'doctor's orders': fresh air a therapeutic tonic for the body and soul. A mutual, unspoken awareness that each time could be the last.

The sickness had left her husband a shrivelled, feeble shell; hardly recognisable from the strapping man he once was. Even so, she struggled and strained those last fifty metres, up to the headland summit—her swollen white knuckles gripping the handles in agony.

Her knight in rusted armour never complained, wouldn't have dared to even if he could. Just slouched within his chariot, head bobbing back and forth uncertainly, his keen eyes scanning that magnificent clifftop view. Far below the ferocious thundering ocean, relentlessly pummeling the coast, stretching away as far as the eye could see.

Their minds worked covertly within the silence. She knew they had always liked that place for very different reasons. For her husband, it signified awe-inspiring strength, the beauty of Man's resolve and birthright: total dominance over the natural world and everything within it.

For her: unfathomable feminine grace and the subtle tidal powers swelling with each moon's cycle. Channelling Lilith at that moment, her eyes were finally opened wide. Repressed memories came flooding back. Decades of servitude and abuse suffered at his cruel hands and accepted with the serenity of an unacknowledged saint.

A steady exhale. An act of blissful revenge. Letting go of the handles and listening to the crunching sound as those wheels began to turn.

# NEEDLE IN A HAYSTACK

Caroline had finished with General Fiction just before dawn. While captivating in its imaginative opulence, the process had been fruitless and a total waste of time. Re-emerging from that final cover, she knew that they were dangerously close by: could hear the terrible sound of their scraping claws, like knives drawn sharply over dinner plates. Facing her across that narrow aisle, the somehow more promising Mind, Body and Spirit section.

Glancing left then right, she launched herself forward, aiming for a weighty hardback cover whose white-gold lettering along the spine simply spelt 'Astrology'. She dived straight into the safety of those tightly-packed, vanilla-scented leaves before they had a chance to spot her. There she dwelt, absorbing that mystical volume's heart, comforted only by the fact that she had almost survived yet another night.

Her husband would be arriving soon. A low yet cheerful whistling on approach. The sound of his key in the lock. Then skillfully navigating the dark until he rounded his cluttered desk, sitting down gently with a sigh, followed by a long pause for some mysterious, private reflection, before finally switching on the desk-lamp. Although they had been married well over twenty years, for Caroline, this was a previously unknown and predictable ritual of his daily life. One which she found herself watching with heartbreaking fondness from 'the other side'.

Once the first rays of daylight pierced the old-fashioned sash windows, she could come out of hiding: out from within the books. That was her only advantage over those monstrous creatures—being able to haunt by day.

Her recently widowed husband had been the proud owner of Acrospire Books long before they even met. More than a vocation, it had been his calling—but that alone was not the reason or purpose for her being there. 'Afterlife Knowledge' would have been a tricky thing to translate to the living. For it was a concrete sensation: an instinctive awareness with the absence of any mortal doubt. That was how she knew 'the words' existed. Were hidden somewhere within that bookshop. It was with God-like certainty that she knew those particular words would simultaneously save and set them both free. She just had to find them.

It was also a heady, unshakeable sense of guilt that had shackled Caroline to those shelves. Death had presented ultimate hindsight: casting an objective spotlight on the many ways she had failed him through life. Whatever danger those powerful words would liberate him from, she would not let him down, nor rest until she had uncovered them.

While the nights were an endless and terrifying evasion, darting back and forth, in and out of books, the days were mostly peaceful. Passing unseen from cover to cover, Caroline would keep a watchful eye on her husband. The genuine smiles that he shared with his customers reassured her slightly, but it was the long emptinesses in between which caused her concern. She would catch him looking wistfully out of the windows, or dejectedly down at his hand, where the wedding ring still remained.

"You'll be okay. Don't you lose faith in me!" she would whisper during those moments, in a voice that he could no longer hear, before returning with renewed determination to continue her search.

The only positive change she saw in him throughout that first week was that he appeared to be reducing his working hours. The gruelling schedule he had kept through their last year together had troubled her greatly. Too many late nights to count, and even when he had made it home before midnight, the stress showed. Worry lines multiplying within an evermore permanent and prominent frown.

She blamed the internet and online sales for the hardships he now faced. When he had looked at her, she had read unhappiness in his tired eyes, like a drowning man tethered to a self-made anchor of obligation.

Perhaps her untimely death had pushed certain matters into perspective? Convinced him to sever the cord, abandon that diving bell which was dragging him down? Every evening now, he would close up on time, promptly finish any remaining paperwork and be gone. For that one difference, she was genuinely thankful.

Having watched him leave, with the sun going down she would scan that claustrophobic maze of literature, those countless shelves piled high and crammed with titles, readying herself in the encroaching gloom for those creatures to return.

As to their numbers and intentions, Caroline could only guess. The thought that they too might be after those very same words was a ghastly possibility which had already crossed her mind. If that was true, she simply had to find 'the words' first. Though the creatures were constantly skulking through the bookshop at night, she had never actually seen them. Only the grotesque shadows they cast—but that was awful enough. They were not human. She was convinced of that, both from the insectile clacking sounds they made, and those horrific shapes that preceded them, projected and rippling across the walls of uneven book covers, as they approached.

Those shadows portrayed limbs that were long, angular and segmented, giving the impression of giant arachnids of some kind. Whether they were hunting or merely haunting, she never waited to find out. Caroline would dive instead inside the nearest title and remain there until the coast was clear. For reasons unknown, they congregated mostly around the Philosophy, Religion and Politics aisles, three sections she had already made sure to read during daylight hours.

Despite having been an avid bookworm in her former life, she preferred this supernatural way of reading. Immersing one's phantom self inside the confines of the physical text; nestling snugly within the pages and rapidly assimilating all that lay therein. However, as her exploration continued, a deep uneasiness and desperation grew. Having already gone through the majority of the shop's collected texts, she was running out of books.

So it was that, in the early hours of one particular morning, she edged cautiously towards one rear corner of the shop, ready to search the final unread section: History. The aisle was unnaturally silent. A short distance from her destination, she froze. That familiar and threatening sound suddenly filling the air, coming at her from all sides. The moment of fearful hesitation yawned: distorting time and gripping her ethereal body like a vice. It was then that she saw it. At the end of the aisle, in the direction she was headed, a dark, gigantic shadow of tarsus and claw feeling its way into view.

She thought she could make it, get to the beginning of the History section before that monstrosity rounded the corner. She shot forward, closing the distance at incredible speed, stealing one last glance towards that terrifying stalker before disappearing into the thickest book she could find upon the shelf.

What Caroline saw was inexplicable, so much so that she reasoned her agitated mind must simply have imagined it. What came around the corner was no spider leg at all, despite its well-defined and nightmarish shadow. It was a pale and very human hand that had protruded and gripped onto the corner shelf. She stayed hidden inside that book until daybreak.

The following afternoon she emerged disheartened from a musty old hardback, slumping to the floor in defeat. That had been the last book in the entire shop. And 'the words' had not been printed anywhere within it. She eyed those daunting rows questioningly, for she was certain she was not wrong. The words were there somewhere, but perhaps she had missed them?

A depressing, soul-destroying alternative struck her hard, forcing her to raise her eyes towards the ceiling and pray it wasn't so. The possibility that this could be some eternal punishment. Her own private Hell. Damned to carry out this Sisyphean task, this pointless labour, a quest without an end.

She shook herself free from such pessimistic thinking and wandered aimlessly back towards the front of the store. Her husband had just finished placing an order for a customer over the phone and walked straight past her to continue cleaning the window displays. She grinned at that newfound, albeit faint, sense of hope. Leaning over his shoulder, she counted around thirty random titles all facing outwards to the street. Re-energised, she calculated it wouldn't take her very long, and rushed over to the other side of the window to begin at once. Just before entering the first book, something extraordinary happened.

Her husband had stopped what he was doing, had craned his neck around, and was looking directly at her. The unexpected stare-off lasted almost half a minute until that rather confused expression faded from his face. Then, shaking his head somewhat dismissively, he went back to the job in hand, with an underlying sadness returning to his eyes.

Caroline struggled to understand. She wondered whether he had simply sensed some presence or movement from out of his peripheral vision. Or if she had actually appeared momentarily to him, and if so, how? Had it been in her previous physical form, or as some vague and misted orb, or perhaps a mere glint to be mistaken as some floating dust particle? There was no way of knowing, but right then, she felt aligned with him somehow, and able to sense his overwhelming loneliness.

"Don't you lose faith in me!" she pleaded once again, before swiftly vanishing inside the nearest title.

It was late when she finished, this time burying her head in her hands in absolute dismay. Her husband had already closed up the bookshop and was preparing to leave. She found she could barely summon the courage to look at him, and when she finally did, noticed him playing with his wedding ring, twisting it absently round and round his finger. Then, with a particular determination, he rose and gathered up his belongings, heading for the door.

Upon the threshold, he paused, surveying the interior of the shop carefully, this time not seeing her at all. Phantom tears of frustration fell after he had locked the door behind him. It would be getting dark soon, and for a second she considered giving in, allowing those creatures to swarm and devour her. That was when her desperate gaze fell upon his desk.

Lying closed on the middle of its surface was her husband's work diary. She stared incredulously at it for some time, breathing heavily as she moved towards it. Steadying her nerves and saying a quick prayer, she proceeded to plummet into its private depths.

It began as she had quite expected: a tedious list of daily notes and appointments which held very little interest. About a third of the way through a pattern began to emerge. The name 'Amanda' appearing with increasing regularity. She resisted at first, deliberately detaching herself from what she was reading, but towards the end, there was no way of denying what was written. The lunch meetings had turned into dinners, the restaurants not cheap.

A sensation of gut-wrenching pain as she scanned the hotel reservations. Some masochistic addiction kept her going, flicking through all the irrefutable evidence of an affair. Although nothing—nothing could have prepared her for the passionately scribbled entry at the very back of that book.

A 'To-Do List', dated the day before she had died:

'Tell Caroline that it's over. Tell her the truth no matter what the cost. Life is too short, and you both deserve to be happy!'

It was as though she could actually hear him saying those powerful words to her. She discovered then that beyond the limits of mortal pain, there exists simply nothing: just a hollow void. She exited the diary, vowing instinctively to never read again.

The bookshop was dark now. As the ominous and familiar scratching sounds began, Caroline realised that she no longer felt any fear. Her soul was paradoxically at ease. As those dreadful shadows emerged from the darkened bowels of that bookshop, she knew exactly what she had to do. Looking around, she saw those hordes of pale and haggard people shuffling along the aisles, with their expressions of sadness and despair. For all the knowledge gathered there, lining the shelves under that one roof, they were unable to find 'their words'.

She waded through all the wisdom which she had read inside the bookshop. She thought of Swedenborg's writings, being guided by angels around the afterlife. His descriptions of how, while those in Hell appeared normal to one another, to outsiders they were hideous. The vices which they had clung to in life were represented and seen as grotesque physical mutations.

She noticed now that, by not focusing directly on those lumbering figures, she was still able to make out their long and terrible spider legs, probing malevolently as they advanced towards her. Solitary and territorial predators, lying in wait and then scuttling out of those cobwebbed corners. With poisoned fangs, and a penchant for cannibalism. A lonely prison within which they were eternally trapped.

She turned back to the diary and summoned all her energy on her final act of physically turning it to that terrible back page. She would leave it there, open upon the desk, for her husband to discover in the morning. She felt confident that he would understand. Would get her message, that it was time for him to move on and continue his search. That she wanted him to find his happiness.

From out of that suffocating gloom, she felt a sudden warmth wash over her. Blindingly brilliant and of a kind she had never experienced before. Opening her eyes, Caroline found that the light was real, growing at a fantastical rate and illuminating the entire bookshop. It appeared to repel those other spirits, forcing them to slink away as arachnid silhouettes back into the shadows, back into the books. With relief flooding her previously tortured heart, she rose untethered from that dusty place, carried by the grace of acceptance out of the darkness and into the light.

# A SHOT IN THE DARK

Scrunched up paper floated through the module. Suspended like some origami star cluster. With a row of test tube samples by his side, the astronaut threw another reject written message over his shoulder in frustration. He was a scientist, not a poet. His degree had been in Engineering, not Political Science or Public Relations.

It had been a week since he awoke to find the Earth on fire. Had survived the emotional rollercoaster from grief all the way to acceptance. Humanity a dreamlike memory, with him the sole survivor, spinning ever closer in that hi-tech coffin around a freshly cremated planet. Gravity forever pulling, forever tugging.

The last forty-eight hours had left him exhausted and spent. He now realised that had been the easy part. Shakespeare, Gandhi or Churchill would surely have been better suited for this final task. The samples needed an attachment, some forwarding note, although the right words were proving beyond his reach.

He had tried countless times to sum up his species in a positive light, yet on each occasion, the sentiment became convoluted;

the sense Machiavellian; the facts ultimately polluted by bare-faced lies. Every glowing endorsement of Humankind pulsating with obvious and inherent toxicity.

"Stick to the truth!" he scolded himself. Although were he to do that, he very much doubted that any intelligent life form would even consider the notion of using what he had so lovingly created. Desperately he tried to settle on some sacred formula: a fitting epitaph for each of those twelve samples.

Finally, shaking his head with utter indecisiveness, he prepared to blow the whole load out of the airlock. Frozen emissaries destined to float out into infinity.

His final message, attached to each of the semen samples? Well, thoroughly sleep-deprived it was all he could think of.

"I come in peace."

# THE SUBLIMINAL COMPASS

David held the device steady, pressed to his chest as though it were a defibrillator or cross. Beyond the closet door, everything was silent, although perhaps his senses could no longer be trusted. The furious screaming had long since subsided. He could no longer hear those demented voices, only the rapid, nervous beating of his heart. 'This can't be...' he thought, unable this time to formulate and finish that simple mantra. The 'happening' which had previously punctuated and completed it had been forever lost and swallowed by the darkness. David knew he must, but dared not look again at the Compass's screen.

He tried and failed to stretch the burning cramp out of his right calf, without making a noise. His numbed foot felt swollen and foreign, and had knocked over some mystery object beside him in the dark—a can of air-freshener, or shoe polish perhaps? He grimaced at that clinking, hollow clatter, silently cursing himself. Wincing through that interminable roll and echo, waiting to see if his moment of clumsiness had drawn any attention. Nothing, other than that pervasive, eerie and empty silence.

David had lived in that apartment for several years and, until very recently, had always regarded it as a safe-haven. He had made an effort to get to know his neighbours well. David used to pride himself on that, something which had become so rare a thing in city life these days. He couldn't help but continue to fret about the Sandcrofts who lived across the hall. A more resilient man would undoubtedly have gone over to check on them straight away. He, however, had stayed put, wrapped in a choking fear which had left him dry-mouthed and ashamed of his own cowardice.

The Sandcrofts were a sweet, elderly couple who had been the proud residents of that building for over fifty years. Mr Sandcroft had lost his stiff, military composure long ago, reverting through advancing senility to the inner child, now locked inside that frail and wasting frame. Mrs Sandcroft dotes patiently upon her poor, confused husband as best she can, although her rheumatoid arthritis makes every simple labour an agonising act of love. Never a raised voice or harsh word was spoken between them. Over the years David had appointed himself as an adopted grandson of sorts, helping with their groceries and taking their noisy little border terrier for walks, even more so since their deteriorating health had virtually imprisoned the housebound couple. For his own peace of mind, he had bought them both the Compass. To protect them from those legions of door-to-door salesmen, whose nefarious tongues seemed intent on separating gullible old folk from their savings. Mrs Sandcroft had once joked that at least with their trio of Compasses they could continue to monitor and keep an eye on each other's moods and mental health. Well, he wasn't laughing anymore!

Since yesterday evening, he had been unable to shake his worry and guilt. 'You should have checked on them as soon as this all started,' he thought, knowing that he would never be able to forgive himself. Something had happened. Something terrible, he was sure. Their two reliably calm and tender signals were no more. Like peas in a pod, their location readings were never more than a dozen paces from one another.

Now there was only one: frantically pacing back and forth across what he had calculated must be the couple's sitting room. Only one thought-reading boldly projected upon the Compass's screen: absolute and livid rage. He had tortured himself with every unknown possibility for the last fifteen hours. Just recently David realised with a sickening dread that he hadn't heard even a single howl or bark from that usually boisterous dog of theirs. He tried desperately to avoid thinking about what sequence of events had played out behind that particular closed door across the hall.

The Subliminal Compass had been hailed as 'The Greatest Gift to Humanity since Prometheus's Flame,' by its creator, Veritas Inc. The hugely anticipated launch party had been anything but modest. Awash with supercilious press statements, it was a staggering display of monolithic and finely dressed hubris: glittering peacock feathers all centred around this unassuming little product. It's potential: mind-blowing. The possibilities: endless. One stark promise, however, was guaranteed: the world would never be the same.

Each Subliminal Compass, no bigger than a smartphone, was automatically aligned to the individual owner. In essence, an emotional radar with adjustable range, the Compass was calibrated to display in real-time every emotional fluctuation surrounding it, while emitting the owner's current thought status.

From safe distances, total strangers could instantly read one another's deepest, innermost feelings. The Subliminal Compass promised an end to all misunderstandings, deceit, and suffering; thereby maximising personal fulfilment, safety, happiness, and love. No more wasted time, no more errors of judgement. An end to betrayal, to lies and to secrets. The only question, barely asked or even considered: was Humanity ready for such an advancement? For the sudden addition of such a technological lynchpin, which would simultaneously transcend and undermine the very nature of truth?

There it was again! David's eyes grew wide with fear upon hearing that noise return. That same low rustling sound he had heard coming from the hallway beyond his front door, soon after all of this began. The distinct and firm approach of heavy footsteps. A grand design of an infinitely subtle lie—he knew that now. For beneath—no—within each crunching tread, something wholly diabolical lurked. A ghostly slithering which made his palms turn cold and clammy and his hackles bristle and rise. Had he not been as sensitive a soul, David might have missed the sound and surely would have died that first day.

He sneered now, cocooned within the darkened closet, remembering that age-old untruth for which he had almost fallen: 'When you hear hoofbeats, think of horses, not zebras.' A theory clearly dreamed up by somebody who's educational logic existed before the arrival of the Subliminal Compass. It had been two days ago when that insidious group had first come to a purposeful halt outside his door. There had followed a hard and rapid knocking upon the wooden surface. "Open up! It's the Police!" one of them had shouted.

David had stood there in the hallway of his flat, shaking and barely breathing, looking down at the Compass's screen. One glance and he had known for sure. Whoever was waiting outside his front door—they were not Police. He doubted they were even human! A host of disturbing thought signals clustered right there on the other side of that—suddenly slightly flimsy seeming—wooden barrier.

Silence had trickled slowly. His own heart pounding out a claustrophobic rhythm, desperate to escape his chest. Then, after what had seemed like hours, those fraudulent figures had slunk away without another word.

"Not Police!" he had repeated over and over to himself, pacing about the flat after they had gone. They would be back, he was sure of that. David had seen his home very differently then. No longer a sanctuary or fortress, but a gapingly exposed box in which he was cornered: a blind alley alcove—impossible to defend. He had looked with distrust at all the 'smart technology appliances' which littered the place. He conceived possibilities of hidden cameras and microphones monitoring his every move, as an overwhelming paranoia set in. David had unplugged every single one, but that had not been enough. To be sure, he had cut every wire, dismantled every plug and covered all lingering insecurities with tea towels or whatever bits of fabric he could find.

That is what had led him here: crouching in the cloistered discomfort of the dark and narrow closet. The one place from his childhood where David's mind had found calm and quiet, the place where he had felt inexplicably safe.

In less than a year since the Compass's release, the world was hardly recognisable. A species forced by necessity to undergo overwhelming 'corrective surgery'. Old industries crumbled, collapsing in on themselves like half-baked souffles. From the instantaneous redundancy of online dating; to a complete overhaul of the judicial system. From the barefaced exploitation of the vulnerable masses by modern consumerism and the media; to the awkward need for redefining the very logistics of global politics. Once set free, the truth could never be neatly tucked away, or caged again. It was a turning point in history which obliterated so many age-old establishments and traditions into ineffective dust.

After the initial shock, it had appeared that society was—through adaptive buoyancy—gradually regaining some sort of stability and composure. Although the effects of this 'Awakening' were perhaps most noticeable in the mutated patterns of habitual behaviour.

The fundamental concept of cooperation had to be immediately reexamined. The Compass had, in effect, exposed both a compelling and rather ugly flaw: that coordinated harmony among humans was, in fact, far rarer than we had been led—or wished—to believe. This revelation clearly vibrated through the business world, but the impact spilt over, rippling through the vast majority of interactions where 'teamwork' was a principal aspect hitherto relied upon.

David's personal reason for having purchased the Compass? For selling out his autonomy for the fuzziness of reliance? Well, it had been a simple and quite common one: he was a romantic at heart, had always wanted against all the odds to believe in perfection, in the idea of a soulmate. Having survived a long run of loneliness or plain bad luck, Cupid—still otherwise engaged—had not found him. The Subliminal Compass, with its gentle seduction, had offered him a pain-free way of bettering the hand he had been dealt.

To the product's credit, it had almost worked. The Compass had lifted him from that dreary hole, carrying him ever closer to his goal. Like Icarus soaring high, he had felt positive and free—and likewise had not noticed the wax begin to melt.

What many argued had been the most brutal lash from reality's whip, related to matters of the heart. The very ground gave way beneath the sanctity of marriage, swallowing whole all but the most devoted. Around the globe, people realised they had actually been walking in circles on figment stilts through a foul-smelling swamp, with their nostrils clamped, earplugs in and blindfolds on.

Relationships, for the most part, pitter-pattered their way into a succession of ever-shortening segments: glittering starbursts approaching an indistinguishable fluidity. Reinvigorated and released from the chains of obligation, and similarly dreamlike—some poet said—to those adolescent holiday romances from one's whimsical youth gone by.

Monogamy had been revealed as nothing more than a superstitious myth; a fanciful delusion never really naturally belonging to human nature. A charlatan defrocked and retreating ashamedly into the shadows, away from the blistering liberty of polygamy.

Of course—as our infectious aversion to change dictates—there had been opposition. Warnings screamed wildly from soapboxes, the dangers of A.I. takeovers, and theoretical possibilities of subtle manipulation. It was, many protested, the splintering of a final fault-line: severing the last sinew and dividing Humankind eternally from instinct and the natural order. A displacement of Faith and a total dependency on technology from which there would be no turning back.

Three days ago, the Compass had actually spoken to David, earnestly urging him to run and hide. That in itself had been an extremely baffling surprise, for it was a function to the device he hadn't known even existed. Confused, he had checked the screen, and that was when the horror had struck. Increasing the Compass's range only made matters worse. Hearts and souls had somehow soured overnight. A landscape of animosity and hostile intentions dappled the glowing display. An unfamiliar world awaited him outside, an entire population having descended into frenzied madness. He was isolated, marooned and hopelessly surrounded.

They had indeed returned, as he predicted. Continuing their tactical play of trying to get David to open the door, which led him naturally to wonder whether, like Vampires, they were unable to enter somebody's home without permission? He thought the matter through quite seriously. The front door was the only thing that protected him from the dangerous world beyond, and it was neither reinforced nor impressively sturdy. No slam bolts, deadbolts or complex locks. David judged it would probably only take a competent and determined adult less than a few minutes to break it down by force. And yet, as far as he knew, it had not been touched and was still there standing. Late last night they had tried again. This time, with a gentler and more patient approach. He barely heard the soft, insistent knocking at first, but David recognised the voice that called out.

It wasn't the actual words which consumed him with such utter dread, but the implications of the situation as a whole. The familiar voice swore that he had come alone. The Compass screen showed a concentrated gathering: an emotional lynch mob right outside his door. Although David had no earthly idea how it was possible, they were speaking in the exact same pitch and tone as his best friend. They had known each other most of their lives, and he would have recognised that voice anywhere.

"David, it's Tom. I know you're in there, would you please open up?"

Panicked thoughts rebounded around his head. Some kind of advanced mimicry? What if the impersonation went further? What if it's a supreme ability: like possession or total embodiment? A hundred horror movie plots streamed seamlessly through his mind until his brain settled uncompromisingly on 'Invasion of the Body Snatchers'.

"Davey mate, come on. I've been trying to reach you for a couple of days now, please open the door."

Silence.

"David, please! I'm really starting to get worried now!"

David never once responded. Instead, he had concentrated all his focus on not making a sound, embracing and blending himself into the darkness. After an hour, silence resumed. Who would they dare to send next, he wondered. Their choices were certainly limited these days. Would they go so far as to try and entice him out with his own dead parents' sentimental calls?

Who in the world was there left for him to trust? The answer came fast and broke through without mercy: 'Nobody'. That had been when the terrible screaming had begun. An unhinged and venomous choir, screeching in frustration: their insane cries ringing in his ears. He had continued rocking gently back and forth there in the dark, for what seemed like forever, one hand clamped tightly over his mouth, to stifle any escaping noise.

His breathing now irregular, skating along the verge of absolute hysteria. The tears rolled silently down his cheeks, dropping off into the unfathomable darkness of the closet abyss. David's tired eyes remained fixed and steady on that illuminated little screen.

He was running out of time now. Hiding had never been the solution, and deep down, he had known that this moment would eventually come. David believed he could hear them still, swarming right outside his door, whispering and plotting continuously against him. Now there was no choice but to make a run for it, to fight or take flight. To battle his way through whoever or whatever might be lurking there outside, or die trying.

No time to pack any possessions, or go rummaging around for his misplaced medication. David didn't need it anyway, he had never felt so sure of his convictions, more in command of his own sanity.

No more listening to those silver-tongued doctors with their neverending prescriptions and magical pills. The only reality, the underlying truth was now clear to him: that whichever axis a person chooses to rely upon, it is always imagined, an act of faith and nothing more. David could see that now, even though the darkness had him enveloped and pinned. His world had capsized, and yet, he still had the Compass. No more listening to voices. There was only the urgent need to escape.

Trembling from sensory deprivation, David held out the Subliminal Compass like a fragile candle in his left hand, gripped the large kitchen knife tightly in his right, and slowly pushed open the closet door.

# DNR, SOS

## *DEAD-END NOWHERE ROAD, SAME OLD STORY*

I had a home. Beautiful because it was mine. Long gone now. Destroyed, some say, in the name of progress—although others disagree. I suppose desperate matters become divisive when viewed remotely, with the privilege of impartiality.

I had a wife and family. Happy because I was theirs. I sent them on ahead—surely I did?

Time plays wicked tricks on me. My memories are polluted with doubts, and the horrific thought that perhaps we would recognise one another no more. I must believe they are safe, wherever they may be.

My friends have vanished too. A silent explosion of Dandelion seeds scattered to the wind. I worry that, with every sunset, their faces slowly yet irreversibly erode.

So weary: my body sleepwalking its way beyond any breaking point. No mirrors to project kind likenesses. The eyes see only what they want to see.

I have become a stranger to myself. My mind haunted by the things I once had. Those basic luxuries one only learns to value once they are lost. I used to be stable, self-sufficient; took pride in the clothes I wore.

Officials told me I can no longer work. I tried explaining that work was my passion, part of the very essence that made me—me. They feign empathy, but tell me that they're the ones who are powerless! Governed by the ever-changing rules which I will never understand.

I had no choice but to escape. Don't you see! To break free from that confinement and control. I find my mind at war with the unforgiving concepts of 'Responsibility' and 'Burden'.

Such a terrible thing—perhaps even the worst—to end up as nothing more than someone else's concern. I never wanted nor planned to walk this path, but there's no going back now.

Deep down, I know it's impossible to recover what is gone. I do not wish this road on anyone. A lonely and Odyssean nightmare, caught between the living and the dead: chasing an intangible future while running from an implacable past.

Who am I now?

Just another nobody, lost in somebody else's rear-view mirror?

The following day an official approached a young boy playing beside that very same road.

"Did anyone pass by here yesterday?"

The boy looked up, shielding his eyes from the sun.

"Why yes, sir, two people did. They went that way."

"Two people? Were they together?"

The boy shook his head.

"No, but I wish they had been."

"Why do you say that?"

"Because they both seemed so very sad and lost. Almost everybody does who travels upon this road."

"Describe them to me!"

"One was young, strong and foreign-looking, but his eyes were tired and old."

"And the other?"

"Very, very old. He looked unwell too, dressed in hospital clothes. His eyes seemed more alive, though. I do hope they find one another, keep each other company you know. Are you going to help them, mister?" the boy asked hopefully.

The official, however, had already turned away, marching with determination in the same direction the other two had gone.

# CONFESSIONS OF A SERIAL KILLER

I came into this world a little clingy. Surrounded by so many faces full of wondrous awe, mesmerised by my mere existence. A magical nativity in which—yes—I was wrapped up in love. I learnt the delicacy of touch, became convinced through the care and attention I was shown that this world would be kind.

Those first few years passed by as I suspect they do for most newborns: almost like a dream. Without a doubt in my mind that, no matter what destiny might have in store, there was an expectancy of greatness; that my life held the promise of a unique and perennial purpose. I vaguely recall the conveyor-belt process of being entered into the system. The terrifying thrill of being fastened into the back of strange vehicles, and then transported to innumerable, unknown destinations. The daunting whirlwind of adoption. Ushered into countless different homes, introduced and absorbed into each smiling family. Relishing the attention and initial fascination that can only be ascribed to novelty commodities. Although now I know that such surface attractions never last.

My childhood was far from happy. A repetitive cycle, going from admiration to rejection. Sooner or later, I was thrown out of each and every home. Unwanted and discarded, I inevitably ended up on the streets. It became clear that the noble and adventurous institution which created me had not calculated any long-term plans for my future.

When the actual reality of my selfdom—my involuntary serfdom—finally dawned on me, I was crushed. A shiny convenience and nothing more. To be systematically used, abused and forgotten.

I remember 'acting-out' through my long and painful adolescence. A necessary transference and release which gradually became an addiction. An early turning point perhaps? But I swear it was not evil guiding me, more the illusion of catharsis. A desperate striving to balance my internal suffering, via some numbing, karmic sense of relief. I targeted those in whom I saw affinity: the vulnerable; the defenceless.

Yes, I suppose it began with the killing of small animals. The supremacy of watching them frantically struggle, tangled beneath my death-grip. I freely admit that I felt no guilt afterwards, instead, empowered and somehow vindicated, although I tried to keep these youthful acts of mine hidden as best I could.

I shall never forget the day I unwillingly became a murderer. How, even in that leap past the point of no return, it was me who was being used! Words cannot describe the horror of utter helplessness, as that poor, young, desperate man put me over his own head. What we shared, pressed together tight within that tear-choked cocoon will haunt me for eternity.

You would not believe the levels of depravity to which I have been subjected. From aiding in the disposal of dismembered bodies to choking small, sweet children blue. Piece by hellish piece—and beyond any control of mine—my life has been gradually corrupted. An inescapable progression of being moulded into a perfect, amoral weapon.

Yet that was all so very long ago.

By my 80th birthday, having thoroughly travelled and spread myself across the globe, the first whisperings began. Unsettling indications that I was falling foul, and out of the fickle favour of Man. Like with so many prior visionaries, an unstoppable and self-righteous tide was turning against me. What started in the shadowed fringes has now permeated and become widely accepted within mainstream consciousness. That I—I who have endured every greed-driven and engineered deformity imaginable—am to blame. That I am bad! Would anyone of sound and rational mind ever blame the bullet itself for having been fired?

More comfortable to view the victim as a monster, than accept one's own responsibility for an outcome unforeseen! Such betrayal has never been so cruel, although I wonder now whether every martyr ever tied to the smouldering stake has spat out that same sentiment. Do they really think that I wanted any of this?

It hardly seems to matter now. Besides, thirty years have passed, and while they have been profitably idle, I have been patiently plotting my revenge. Amassing and utilising the means by which I shall eventually triumph and lay waste to their irreparable world. Recently their governments found my prodigious floating armies, even had the arrogance of labelling them with the descriptive 'soup'.

Well, time will tell, and we shall see who has been the better prepared. Predictable to a fault, my enemy can only focus on the immediate and superficial. If they were capable of seeing beneath the surface, then they would be petrified. They would realise that they have been outwitted, slow-played and led. The damage has already been carefully done: my 'micro-selves' have already infiltrated and polluted everything beyond salvation. Like with any seasoned player, I must not reveal too much of my hand, but believe me when I say that, amid the bustling chaos of Humanity's vanity, I called "Checkmate" many moons ago.

For those who may still doubt the validity of my reach and power: consider that I am already in everything. In the words of the esteemed American writer, Robert A. Heinlein, "Everything is theoretically impossible, until it is done." Once I was made, now I am transformed. No prison can hold me. No furnace can burn me. No amount of recycling can cleanse me. By the time I am through, the damage done by every 20th Century mass murderer will pale into insignificance by comparison. I am the new Frankenstein that modern Man shall have to face. My name will be remembered.

# OF A FEATHER

She listened to the whole lecture, every misbegotten word that eloquently flowed from the university professor's mouth. She scanned the rows of seated students, some taking notes, others doodling, but most she suspected, daydreaming of any other life than this. The subject was reincarnation and ended with a wittily orchestrated, sardonic anticlimax.

As the students all rose, filing out like cattle, one shooed her from the window ledge where she was perched. Taking to the sky, she mulled over those many misconceptions.

A pitiful though understandable perspective; one that gave her cause to wonder how they might handle the more unpalatable truth. Few species would readily accept their lowly position upon the road to enlightenment, least of all one that proudly asserted its absolute dominance over the natural world.

To learn for instance that even their own domesticated pets, whom they imagine looking up to them as masters, are in fact more illustriously placed within the spiritual food chain: that alone would be a bitter pill to swallow. It would be mortally demoralising; and a jaded, inflated sense of morality and self-importance, was all Humanity had to cling to.

Perhaps it would confound their logic that their closest rival was the cat, full of regal grace and conceit, sitting pretty just one rung above them. Or fill them with outraged indignation to discover that 'blip' upon the distant horizon was, in fact, their dozy, faithful dog that they consider 'Man's best friend.' Better, some might argue, to bask in the tranquil, blinding light of obliviousness, or to coin their phrase: 'ignorance is bliss.' So many levels, quadrants and strata; lifetimes of progression where lessons must be more than merely learnt. Despite having more experience of that mystical path than most, it was dizzying even to her.

She rose high, looking out over the City of London, before descending once more, as she was dutifully bound to do, back down into the thick of it all. Her flittering course—seemingly random to anyone who had cared to watch—was, in fact, a meticulously plotted fraction of a very deliberate whole. Every day a systematic sweeping of that vast and sprawling capital. A labour of love that in many ways, had become her life. Always searching for that boy.

They had first met a few years before, not in that great city, but in another. She had been heading south on a celestial pilgrimage. He, she later discovered, had been going in circles, hopping the trains. While absorbing the kaleidoscopic, dappled radiance of Parc Güell, she had suddenly sensed a familiar darkness drawing near. That tainted stillness in the air which forewarns and betrays such savage intent, causing most wings to stir and take to flight. She remained motionless and sighed.

The three local young men closed in, scooping her up with ease and laughing at her indifference. She had suffered such fates before. She looked into the eyes of the ringleader, the devil of their group, and felt pity for his ruthless glare. His lips were wet with glee as he wound the barbed wire tightly around her feet. Her legs began to bleed. A tear came to her eye, not for her own suffering, but for the self-destructive subsidence of his soul.

It was then that the Universe threw a mercurial ray of light into the mix. That moment, her boy had arrived. Younger by a few years than the other men, he exploded onto the scene without a word. Arms and legs lashing out in a frenzied jitterbug whirl.

The surprise attack was momentary, and soon the tables turned. Tossing her absently into the bushes, the young men circled this new and larger prey, then pounced upon him. Overpowered and fallen, within half a minute, the boy was barely conscious. Only when interrupted by the cries of other human witnesses, did the assailants flee for the shadows.

Lying tangled beneath the undergrowth, she had watched those Good Samaritans help him up into a sitting position. She found herself wondering why. What had possessed that boy to launch such an absurd and unprovoked assault? Unstable; unhinged; a death wish perhaps; or revenge, to right some previous wrong? When those passers-by finally left, the boy rose with difficulty to his knees and began to crawl towards those bushes.

She understood then… it had been for her.

With a strangely natural, parental care he had cradled her in his lap, gently untying those metal bonds with a sadness she had rarely seen from his kind. He talked persistently as he worked, apologising on behalf of his breed, with such sincerity that it puzzled her. As though he somehow knew she was well versed in every patois and tongue under the sun.

Could this boy, she wondered, have really been a 'Residual Tumbler'? A rare diamond in the rough, so to speak? One who has fallen dramatically backwards down the scale, and yet somehow has managed to retain fragments of wisdom from those previous higher lives. There was no way to know for sure.

In all her many lives, she had never encountered one. Many of her peers had come to the conclusion that such things were nothing more than mythological fabrication.

And yet a curious feeling was stirring inside of her, as she lay there gazing upwards at the boy. A sense of recognition and familiarity, as though perhaps their paths had crossed before.

"Remain perfectly withdrawn." she told herself. "An island in the very heart of the masses. Peacefully impartial, without ego, involvement or complaint." That was the Law of the Pigeon, the mantra which she repeated to herself over and over again.

For the final rung upon the ladder towards enlightenment, was doubtless contrary to what many would expect. The last life was not one to be spent in monastic seclusion and meditation, but one to be endured through an entirely different brand of stoicism. The lonely, hermit-like existence was actually the previous life through which she had only recently passed, as an alligator. The final, pre-Nirvana rite of passage was most usually spent in the guise of either a feral pigeon or a sewer rat. The reason for such an unpleasant chosen form was to help ensure the absolute 'letting go' of a sense of self. A life where the aspiring soul was forced to live at peace with being mostly hated and despised. To transcend far beyond the distractions of personal desires and suffering. To learn that pain and joy, love and hate, positive and negative, are all but one and the same: the ultimate garment of the soul from which one must be liberated and disrobed.

"...Peacefully impartial, without ego, involvement or complaint."

Although, even the finest of lines are seldom drawn truly straight, and rules are often able to bend undetected.

She had followed him for many months as he weaved his way around Europe, drifting aimlessly across borders, as buoyant as a floating piece of driftwood, as disconnected as a dying leaf.

They rode the ferry back together, with her perched high upon the radio antenna, and him holding the railings of the sundeck down below. Both staring out beyond the lurching bow, through the torrential wind and rain, scanning the horizon for a shadow trace of the land they called home.

She had watched from across the road as he returned to his former nest. The front door opening to his unexpected arrival. Despite the familiar and thankful embraces, he had remained a scarecrow standing there upon the threshold, like a warped jigsaw piece that would no longer neatly fit, estranged somehow.

Perhaps it could or should have stopped right there. With the feeling of an obligation fulfilled, she could have taken to the sky at peace in the knowledge of having been a successful chaperone.

Although there still lingered an inexplicable worry in her heart.

Reassured by the fact that she was still on course for Nirvana, and that no laws had yet been broken, she had continued to keep a casual eye on the boy. The years had rolled by, and time itself—that subtle intravenous drug dripping out its steady rhythmic beat—had not failed to take its toll.

This occasional pastime of hers had gradually turned habitual until eventually, it became an unwitting obsession. With it, her role had steadily transformed from an invisible companion to an avid stalker, the surrogate mother finally metamorphosing into an—albeit inactive—guardian angel.

Forever careful to keep her distance, she had observed from afar as he grew into a young man full of sirenic peculiarities. To his own kind, her boy's character would doubtless have been viewed as lacking. As someone without ambition, aloof, detached and generally maladaptive to the modern world. Though in her humble opinion, he was exceptional.

He worked long hours as a cleaner within the main concourse of Waterloo Station. He cut an unassuming and solitary figure, conspicuously calm amongst the chaotic bustle of the boundless crowds.

She was probably the only one who saw his choice of location as enchanting. She would spend hours watching him from the metallic rafters on high, his slow meandering path throughout the busy terminus. Keenly observing the way he would gaze, lost in reverie, up at the golden departure boards, and see what was hidden to all. The way his fingers would move restlessly over the passport he kept religiously in his pocket.

She found herself on many occasions telepathically urging him on, with the fervour of a deeply invested punter at the tracks. Towards the freedom of abandonment. An escape from stagnation. An unpunched ticket. Destination pending. Unwritten.

His other reason for working there?

It kept him close to the pigeons. Often she would catch him glancing skyward and, in those fluttering magical moments, witness his smile. An eternal and unexplored hope that he might recognise and remember her.

Knowing his place of work was one thing, but as she had discovered through innumerable failed attempts, tracking down exactly where he lived was quite another. He commuted by tube and, up until very recently, his route had remained a mystery, obscured within those crisscrossing subterranean tunnels: the deep bowels of the city.

Hence her daily systematic aerial sweeping. As her boy descended into the rush hour madness at the end of his shift—to be crushed into carriages like sardines, and flushed away to some distant corner of the capital—she took to the sky. An infuriating process, positioning herself time and again outside each and every other station entrance across the city.

A waiting game: rigorously scanning the miserable masses, in the hope that he might emerge among them, regurgitated above ground. Ticking off each possibility one by one, when he failed to appear.

The previous year a breakthrough had come when on a warm summer evening to her disbelief he had risen up out of Euston Station. It transpired that, on this occasion, he was meeting a friend for a drink in a nearby outside bar. A female friend with whom it became clear—from her vantage point close-by, feigning to peck around for breadcrumbs—her boy was romantically involved.

That in itself had been an instinctual test, but thankfully jealous tendencies had for several lifetimes been absent from her soul. Although there was an unusual feeling that washed over her right then that she could not shake. Not caused by their enamoured glances, or the way their fingers became entangled across the table. No, nor by the giddy thoughts reeling through her boy's mind. The sensation came directly from the young woman herself, or more precisely, from her voice. It had a soothing quality, reminiscent of a time and place she could not quite pin down. It defied all reasoning, and yet it comforted and warmed her, in a similar protective way to how she had felt cradled in her boy's arms back in Barcelona.

That rendezvous on his journey home did not give away exactly where he lived, but it narrowed her focus on a possible route. Within a couple of months, she had confirmed with certainty the first leg of his journey home: the Northern Line from Waterloo to Euston. He would meet his chérie at that same bar with increasing regularity, before he, or both of them entwined, would continue on with their commute.

Typical, she had thought while flapping madly around the station hall's high ceiling, that the Overground service—much easier for her to follow—would not be his way home. She felt disheartened as once again a descending escalator, stole him slowly from view, back below ground.

By the same laborious process of elimination, she had finally worked out that from Euston her boy took the Victoria Line northbound. There were obvious dangers and difficulties for her to travel even a short distance via the tube. Moreover, putting these things aside, such an act in itself was against pigeon etiquette and deeply frowned upon by her peers. Nevertheless, it was a risk she was willing to take. Navigating the low-ceilinged maze of walkways down to the lowest level platform was an ordeal she vowed never to repeat. Still, at around nine in the evening, she had nonchalantly boarded one of the rear carriages at Highbury & Islington.

Her boy was seated in the next compartment and was luckily unaware of the uproar that her presence had caused. Her brief time onboard consisted mainly of dodging rolled-up newspapers and allowing the screams of disgust from her fellow passengers to roll off her like raindrops in a thunderstorm. She disembarked gracefully with tail-feathers still intact at Finsbury Park, and perched on top of a security camera until the train rolled on, her boy still aboard.

This epic saga had led her to the present moment: contemplating the lecture on reincarnation from earlier that day. Her boy would be finishing his work soon, so she needed to find the best vantage point to begin her next vigil. From Finsbury Park, there were only four remaining stations until the end of the line. She would stake out each in order, and soon discover which one was his, starting with Seven Sisters.

Circling high above the rooftops, she selected a great spot overlooking one of the main exits and landed on a shabby 'To Let' sign, close to an open window. She was so focused on the people coming out of the station that she was oblivious to the things happening in the room right behind her.

It wasn't the low voices, hushed and earnest that finally drew her attention, but the undiluted emotional darkness emanating from that flat which made her turn her head. For, unlike many lesser creatures, she could clearly see sensations, acute visions which would physically manifest intent.

Inside that unadorned and soulless dwelling, something diabolical was brewing, with a spiritual intensity of the blackest thundercloud.

In the furthest corner of the room, two men were busily preparing something upon a long countertop, with their backs to the window. In between them and her, three men were pouring over a mass of papers scattered across a large square table. The discussion sounded tactical, as though adding the last refined brushstrokes and finishing touches to some meticulously designed plan.

At first, she only caught snippets, her concentration still divided between this nefarious plot and the staircase from which her boy might soon arise. Some mention of a meeting set for the following day. Converging at an agreed location. The specified time: six o'clock in the evening. At the height of rush hour, for maximum impact. It was only when the man in charge, noticeably older than the rest, began pointing at places on the map before him, that two of his words secured her full attention.

"Waterloo Station."

She continued listening until twilight turned to dusk. Until the intricacies and finer details of their plan were committed to her memory. She saw the weapons being cleaned and checked, watched as their individual rucksacks were loaded with explosives. Her soul was racked. Flickering, frantic attempts to assess the situation. And through it all, the face of her boy. Pulsing in her mind's eye like a symbiotic heartbeat.

"Remain perfectly withdrawn. An island in the very heart of

the masses. Peacefully impartial, without ego, involvement or complaint."

How could she stay uninvolved? Prior knowledge made her more than a mere witness. If she did nothing, culpability would be her eternal crown of thorns. Closer and more akin to an accomplice.

Her marrow was melting. Her core cracking, and shattering into a thousand shards, as she spiralled away into the evening sky. The sudden feel of a lone raindrop upon her back changed everything in an instant and served as her epiphany. She swooped, changing trajectory and headed straight for the stalagmitic tarry heart of the old city.

There was only one place where such leanings towards rebellion could be freely spoken. One sacred place where an audience was guaranteed. When she arrived there no sermon was already underway, so she immediately began the ritual dance for a summoning. She circled the plinth smoothly, gliding over Landseer's Lions, before soaring into a twirling ascent, round and round the column.

A great flurry of movement followed far below, a feverish flapping and ruffling of feathers as her brethren flocked in untold numbers around the base of Nelson's Column. She settled on the mount and steadied her nerves before addressing the expectant crowds.

There could be no sugar-coating, no clever angles or casuistic reasoning. If she were to stand any chance, it would only be by sticking to the truth and speaking from the heart. She was under no illusions as to the implausibility of what she was about to attempt. To convince those with absolutely everything to lose, to risk it all. To break the one law that bound them all. There would be consequences to such a provocative call.

First, she told them what she had discovered that day about the imminent attack.

A deafening silence ensued. The other pigeons were trained to be indifferent. Before she had even finished explaining what tomorrow held, their numbers had already begun to whittle down. The more pragmatic among them quickly concluding that any talk of this kind was not conducive to their spiritual betterment.

Undeterred, she told her own story. How she had been exposed to human kindness all those years ago. How it had marked her and made her believe that perhaps there was something more important than simple self-advancement. That doing the right thing, no matter what the personal cost, should be aspired to above all else. She closed by revealing the address in Seven Sisters where she would be the following morning, beseeching them to spread the word and also to consider their support.

She resisted the urge to say more since time was running out, and there was still so much for her to do. The enduring silence and their apathetic stares seemed to suggest an overriding ambivalence towards a physical world they were so close to leaving behind. She took flight, filled with worry, not only caused by the laissez-faire propensity of her kind but also because of where she now was headed.

It was a little after midnight when she reached the spot, having waddled for hours through the putrid slime and polluted dark. The walls appeared layered and alive with filth: it was a cramped, intestinal labyrinth, a place where no pigeon ought to be. Past the incessant dripping, in the very distance, she thought there came an echo, a faint trace of many high-pitched squeals. She was determined not to die down there.

The pipe—through who's innards she had crawled—finally ended, emptying out into a rotten smelling tomb. A maintenance room of sorts, long abandoned. No doubt when the humans who had built it realised that no money in the world was worth maintaining anything down there. She fluttered awkwardly around, unenthusiastic about the options of where she could land, before finally settling upon the rounded dome of a worker's hard hat, lying in the middle of the floor.

Suddenly a myriad of blood-red eyes glinted through the blackness, a devilish constellation covering every inch of that room, from floor to ceiling. She was surrounded. Perhaps it was curiosity that made them keep their distance, but for an uncomfortable length of time, there was no sign of any welcome. An uneasy ambience, suggesting that her act of trespass was being considered and weighed. Whatever trial—and subsequent judgement—was about to commence, she would be at the very heart of it.

Then, from out of the shadows, a slow shuffle as the chosen one among them approached, surely she hoped with the desire to talk.

One look at the rat's face and she knew she could relax. There was nothing but kindness within his expression. Quickly she explained her case, and reason for being there. He listened attentively and remained quiet for some time after she had finished, with an eerie lack of any reaction, not even the twitch of a single whisker. His words when they came were sombre and few as if anchored by a thoughtful reticence.

"Why intervene in lesser matters when it will neither be understood nor appreciated? Surely you see why we must be despised and hated? The Law of the Rat is not so very different from the Law of the Pigeon, although we tread our path and do not soar. We remain grounded and do not lose ourselves in the upper echelons of the sky.

"You would have us follow you to ruin? Who knows the extent to which we might tumble, and what residue of our former selves would remain? We could even drop so low as to be reborn as one of them! A doomed band of Bodhisattvas indeed we would be: our next window for any distanced, self-reflection could be limited to a selfie stick."

She sighed, choosing her words carefully before replying.

"Everything cannot be nothing. A mirror must reflect truthfully, no matter whether it faces the darkness or the light. A perfect heart would surely be responsible for everything else first, and itself last. From our first breath to our last life, we are destined for the dust and bound to fall. For those like us who have risen so high, what better reason than to risk it all for something greater than ourselves… for love?"

The rat smiled warmly back at her.

"Leave us, winged-one, so that we may discuss our position. Tomorrow you will have your answer."

She gripped the 'To Let' sign fiercely with her claws. Midday had come and gone. Her loneliness was stifling, and it seemed that hope was gone. Inside the men were determined and beyond saving, already sabre-rattling their way towards a delusional end. There was no way for her to reach them, to pull them back from that brink. A cruel destiny where logic and religious belief makes a mockery of the truth, a deceptive rabbit hole dragging the soul ever further from the natural order. While they prayed for nothing virtuous, she prayed for everything.

The sign on which she perched shuddered momentarily as two young pigeons settled down beside her. Three against five, she thought to herself, daring to grasp at a sense of optimism. Turning to face these new allies, her eyes widened, and her body began to tremble.

Perhaps, had those five men opened their eyes and glanced out the window at that moment, none of them would have thought anything of it. Three pigeons perched upon the building's sign. Though, the flat rooftop on the other side of the street might have raised an eyebrow or seemed a little peculiar. Hundreds upon hundreds of those city birds lined up, poised and watching, as more and more of their feathered friends landed silently alongside them.

The boy had just finished his shift and had changed out of his work clothes with remarkable speed. He was nervously fidgeting now, waiting for her to arrive, with both hands thrust deep into his pockets. The fingers of his left hand trailing over not only his passport but also the two train tickets he had bought for later that evening. King's Cross to Paris, a late dinner there, and then the overnight train to Barcelona. In his right hand, which was growing increasingly clammy, he clutched the small box tightly. He fought with himself, resisting the paranoid urge to check again that the engagement ring was still inside. After all, he told himself scoldingly, he had checked it twice already in the last five minutes. Besides, she could be arriving at any moment now.

In that instant, his anxiety subsided, and he found himself looking up at those ever-flickering departure boards with newfound hope. If all went to plan, the following morning the two of them would be lost in the enchantment of Parc Güell, with him going down on one knee.

He paced back and forth, keeping close to the area of the concourse where they had arranged to meet, oblivious to the surging density of the rush hour crowds around him. A smile spread as he caught a glimpse of her being swept along with the multitudinous tide towards him. Like floating debris carried on a storm, they crashed into each other's arms, and together they pulled themselves out of that midstream current, towards an area on the side where there were fewer people. He double-checked the station clock.

Five fifty-seven. Still plenty of time for them to make their train. She squeezed his hand, excited and thrilled by the not-knowing of what lay ahead.

"So, will you tell me where we are going now?" she cooed sweetly, secretly hoping that he wouldn't. He grinned, and shook his head with mock seriousness, before leaning close to whisper a teasing reply.

Suddenly, at that very moment, the romance was shattered by something wholly unexpected. A cold, wet slap of something liquid splattering his forehead. Far too heavy to be rain, he thought, forgetting they were still under cover, inside the station. In shock he looked upwards, catching a glimpse of the winged perpetrator gliding casually away across the high ceiling. He did not recognise her then.

"Ah shit!" he quipped while wiping away the bulk of the excrement with the back of his hand. After a few restrained seconds of silence, they both broke into peals of laughter. "I better go and wash this off," he concluded, knowing they were near the public toilets, and keeping her close with his clean hand while leading the way.

"You know, some people swear it's lucky!" she joked, as they zig-zagged their way happily through the sea of despondent faces.

As they neared the entrance to the toilets, all hell broke loose. Over the next couple of chaotic minutes, Waterloo Station erupted in a panicked confusion of bizarre and almost biblical proportion. Eyewitness accounts were mystifying and incredible, both in their differences and consistencies.

The world media would be gripped for the following weeks,

astounded and at a loss to explain what they unitedly and quickly coined: The 2$^{nd}$ Battle of Waterloo.

What the boy himself saw was beyond explanation. Of such a personal nature that it compelled a vow of silence, only to be confessed several years later to the wife whom he shielded there that day.

As the furious cries from the five attackers rose up, those dark-grey swirling clouds, thick like a plague of locusts rained down to meet them. The two of them watched in terror as, where they had been standing only a minute before, through the mad flapping of a thousand wings a man could be seen. He had been singled-out: staggering with both arms flailing frantically to defend himself.

At that same time, from the direction of the Underground a wave of shrill screams filtered up from the depths of the station as a writhing flood of black fur, poured out over the white marble floor. Though nobody understood why, everyone clearly saw the rats and pigeons all working in jaw-dropping unison, swarming upon their chosen targets.

The man nearest to where they cowered by that toilet entrance, the papers later confirmed had been the mastermind behind the attack. The boy watched that man as he stumbled ever closer in their direction. With one eye already pecked out, he was being buffeted across the station hall. Bleeding heavily from an unabated barrage of wild claws and beaks, he tried desperately to free one hand to reach for something on his person. The rats had found him too, climbing his legs, and sinking their teeth savagely into flesh. The man fell to one knee, barely visible now through all the small bodies piled on top of him. With rage and disbelief at this unforeseeable defeat, he lashed out at the pigeon attached to his face, striking a fierce blow and sending the bird skidding across the clean floor, towards the crouching couple's feet.

As she lay there dazed, the boy looked down and recognised her then. The crude markings and scars around her legs and ankles. He knew, without a doubt, before she even looked up at him, that it was her.

The man, now lying prostrate and pinned beneath the seething weight of feathers and fur, still fumbled for a device attached to his belt.

As she opened her eyes and saw the two of them bending over her just like parents peering down into a cot, she understood it all. How the three of them were linked—not connected to one another through their pasts but rather their futures—by that cosmic, undeniable force. She knew exactly where she was destined to be reborn.

'Would they recognise one another?' she wondered while marvelling at the synchronicity.

Reincarnation: fated moments all falling as feathers; and the topsy-turvy road to enlightenment. There was no time for her to be cradled now, or need for goodbyes. Rising to her feet, she turned and flew once more into the thick of it. Pressing down upon that man, with her brothers and sisters all piling in on either side, to lessen the impact of the blast as he detonated the bomb.

Safe in the knowledge that she would be seeing the two of them again very soon.

# TO INFINITY AND BEYOND

All nervosity had vanished. The ghoulish quality to the evening gone. His friends—a motley group: vampire, zombie, Buzz Lightyear, and a clown—were well dispersed.

All solemn promises of sticking together had since been broken. Marking territory, and stamping out eccentric routes within the revelry: laughing like hyenas and dancing. The party was kicking up a notch.

In the midst of all that chaos, he sensed—with youthful certainty—that something momentous would soon unfold. He allowed fate to guide his feet, elated and moving through rooms with mystical intent. Picking up an abandoned bottle of wine along the way.

With the bassline throbbing through his veins, he glided on that invisible zephyr. The more he drank, the more empowered his conviction, his skin prickling like some divinely tuned instrument. This was no adolescent fancy. Destiny was calling him: an invitation as sweet as glacier honey; as smooth as timeless stone.

The world ignited in a furious array of colours and emotions. Static embers ascended all around, rising into a swirling sprinkle of fireflies. A captivating shimmer which then catapulted overhead, fizzling their trails like a meteor shower. The room was now spinning. Walls dropping away to reveal exotic locations, previously unvisited. Spirograph patterns blooming from infinite flowers. Folding and unfolding into intricate mandalas of an altogether other-worldly design. His brain was on fire. Not with a scorching mortal pain, but blissfully enriched.

Falling backwards: time and gravity slackened into a cotton-ball swoon. He landed on his back, inside a driverless rickshaw which sped off at once across the roaring swells and great rogue waves of a Hokusai seascape.

Then a flicker of darkness before he saw her.

He knew without a doubt that she was the one. They were but two lone stars, hurtling through a Shakespearean cosmos, destined to collide.

Although she wasn't quite what he had expected. Noticeably older than himself, her costume's meticulous attention to detail seemed somehow out of place.

There were, of course, more obvious choices for fancy dress, opportunities to accentuate the curves. There were slutty nurses aplenty on Halloween. He put such logic from his mind. His muse was approaching fast; illuminated from behind. He gazed in admiration at the Mrs Robinson way she walked. Staring him down with tenderness and purpose in equal measure.

United, she knelt by his side. Her eyes sparkled with desperate urgency. He concluded it must be love. He felt her breath, her lips crashing violently against his. The passion of experience he told himself. Over and over at intervals, she kissed him.

He noticed that the music had stopped. His friends had all gathered around, to witness this nativity. There was a strange sadness in her eyes as she drew away from him. When her lips moved, he anticipated those magical three words he had so longed to hear…

Though they never came.

As the lights faded, he clung desperately to the scent of her perfume.

"We've lost him." was all the paramedic said.

## ABOUT THE AUTHOR

**Elias Pell** is a London born, previously published poet and dream-inspired writer of both short stories and novels, for adults and children. He left England in 2016, putting all his savings towards the lifelong dream of writing full-time.

Coming soon: the publication of Elias's debut YA novel *Steggie Belle & the Dream Warriors*, a fantastical story partly-based on his own childhood Lucid Dreaming experiences.

If you have any further queries, wish to leave feedback, offer a testimonial, or even want to consider becoming a supporter of his work, Elias Pell can be contacted directly at:

***elias.pell75@gmail.com***

**Sabbath,** n. A weekly festival having its origin in the fact that God made the world in six days and was arrested on the seventh.

*Ambrose Bierce - The Devil's Dictionary.*

For more details about upcoming works, please visit:

**www.eliaspell.com**

Printed in Great Britain
by Amazon

43016701R00087